SILVERTIP'S SEARCH

Arizona Jim Silver had to find Rap Bender, Judge Bender's missing son—the same Rap Bender who had joined guns with Silver's oldest and deadliest enemy. But when the legendary Silvertip finally caught up with Bender, they shared a common enemy—ever since Bender's partner double-crossed him by trying to kidnap his woman.

Now it was up to the two men to catch the man Silver had pledged to kill—for Silver's honor and his life!

SILVERTIP'S SEARCH

Max Brand®

GUNSMOKE

First published in the UK by Hodder and Stoughton

This hardback edition 2008
by BBC Audiobooks Ltd
by arrangement with
Golden West Literary Agency

ISBN 978 1 405 68203 9

British Library Cataloguing in Publication Data available.

Printed and bound in Great Britain by
CPI Antony Rowe, Chippenham, Wiltshire

SILVERTIP'S SEARCH

CONTENTS

I

The Judge's Visitor

JUDGE BRENDER had a wooden leg. That was why he refused to let his wife get up and answer the knock at the front door of the ranch house; he always wanted to show that in spite of a wooden leg he was about as active and agile as ever.

So he waved his wife back to her newspaper—it was the idle hour of a mid-morning on Sunday—and he swung himself on his crutches and his sound leg into the hallway. The judge was a big man, but he found himself scowling through the screen door and the blinding light of the day at a man fully as tall as himself. The visitor was big and brown and handsome, and he wore a faint and amiable smile as he took off his hat.

"Are you Judge Brender?" he asked.

The judge, now that the man's hat was off, could see a pair of gray spots in the hair of the stranger above the temples. They looked like horns pushing out through the hair. He never had seen a more peculiar or characteristic marking.

"I'm Brender. Who are you?" demanded the judge.

"My name is Silver. I saw an ad in a newspaper saying that you wanted a man. I dropped in to find out what it was all about."

"I want a man who can ride, shoot, and tell a lie," said the judge. "But I'm tired of talking to men who want the place. Some of them can ride; some of them can shoot a little; but there ain't a one in the lot that's worth anything when it comes to brains. Are you any different from the rest of the lot?"

"Do you want me to tell you how clever I am?" asked the stranger.

The judge considered him with a scowl that grew a little less black. After a while he said:

"Well, come on inside."

Silver stepped into the hallway. The judge noticed two things about him. The first was that the screen door, which usually screamed on its rusty hinges, made no sound as Silver drew it open and closed it behind him. The second thing the judge noticed was that the step of Silver, in spite of his size, made no noise on the squeaking, thin boards of the floor.

The judge put one and one together, and guessed at a million. He knew from that moment that his guest was no ordinary man, and a dim hope began to flicker up into the judge's mind.

"Step into the front room," he said.

Silver laid down his hat, brushed his hair smooth with the flat of his hand, and gave a look at the mask of a huge grizzly bear which was mounted on the wall near the stairs. Then he stepped into the front room. He paused near the door and bowed to Mrs. Brender.

"Name of Silver," said the judge by way of introduction. "He's come about that business. You scatter, Martha, because I gotta waste a coupla minutes finding out what he don't know and why he won't do."

She looked at Silver and shook her head with a smile, apologizing for the roughness of this talk, and silently begging Silver to make allowances. He smiled in return as she shook hands, and then she went out of the room, saying at the door into the hall:

"Mr. Silver had better stay for lunch. There's a mighty good roast of pork in the oven."

"He ain't likely to be staying for no lunch," said Judge Brender grimly.

Mrs. Brender made with her thin hands a gesture of surrender, and disappeared.

"You don't need to sit down and get a chair all dusty," said the judge. "Not till I find out if you can do the first part of the job. Can you shoot?"

Silver shrugged his shoulders, while Brender looked about him as though in search of a proper target right in the room. Then he nodded toward a window.

"There's a three-strand barbed-wire fence out yonder. Cut them three strands with a revolver. Can you do that?"

Silver turned. The wires were glimmering lines of light—dotted lines.

"With a rifle. Not with a revolver," he said.

The judge grinned.

"Well," he said, "there's a pair of birds just lighted on the top strand. What about them?"

Silver walked to the window.

"I'll try," he said.

His back was to the judge, who therefore could not see the movement that drew the revolver. He could not see the gun at all, in fact, and he only knew that the weapon was not leveled shoulder-high, but fired a little above the height of the hip.

At the first explosion, one of those birds on the fence dissolved into a puff of gray feathers. The second dipped off the wire as another shot was fired, then flirted up into the air, unharmed by the bullet, gathering speed. The third shot followed right on the heels of the first pair, and the second bird was blotted out by the big slug of lead.

Silver turned, with his revolver already out of sight beneath his loosely fitted coat. He was not smiling.

"You missed with one of them shots," said the judge, making himself scowl. "Out of practice, are you?"

"I'm never out of practice," said Silver.

"Satisfied with that sort of shooting, are you?" asked the judge.

"Perfectly," said Silver.

The judge wanted to smile, but he controlled himself.

"Well, sit down and rest your feet," he said.

Silver sat down.

"You can shoot," said the judge. "We'll see later about the riding. Now I'm going to find out what you got in your head."

He fell straightway into a long silence.

Silver first looked out the window and saw a pair of gray geldings gallop into view across the nearest field and out of sight again, the sunlight shimmering and winking on the silk of their flanks.

After that he glanced around the room at several enlarged photographs which hung in their frames against the striped paper of the walls. Since the silence continued, he opened an album of old family photographs and ran rapidly through it.

He was closing it when the judge asked:

"What am I thinking about?"

"Your son," said Silver.

The judge started to rise, forgetful that he needed crutches for that purpose. So he toppled a little to the side before he grabbed the crutches, steadied himself, and then thrust his body more deeply into the chair. He grunted loudly.

"You been around making questions of the people before you come to see me?" he asked.

"No. I never have mentioned your name to a soul," said Silver.

The judge narrowed his eyes. He hated a lie.

"But you know I got a son, all the same?" said he.

"Yes," said Silver.

"All right, if you know that much, tell me what he looks like."

"More than medium height, dark eyes, black hair, very handsome. And he seems to be on tiptoe, ready for a start at any time."

The judge glanced absently toward the wall, then back at his guest.

"And you never seen him?"

"No," said Silver.

"And you never talked to anybody about him?"

"No. Not a word."

"All right, all right," said the judge impatiently, making a gesture to clear the atmosphere. "You might go on ahead and tell me about what kind of a boy he is—since you can sit the picture of him right in the air, so to speak."

"Well," said Silver, "he loves fast horses and hunting. Big game and a close shot is his idea of sport. He holds his fire to the last second. He likes poker—when the stakes are high. And he doesn't care what company he keeps, so long as it's exciting."

"Damn!" exploded the judge. "And you mean to tell me that you never seen him or talked about him to nobody?"

"Never," said Silver.

"Where is he now?" asked the judge, holding himself in.

"In disgrace," said Silver. "And you want to get him home. That's why you advertised for a man who can shoot straight and who has a brain to work with."

"By thunder," cried the judge, "you're going to sit there

and lie and tell me you never seen my boy, and never talked about him to nobody?"

"Never," said Silver with his faint smile.

"What's his name?" asked the judge.

"That I don't know."

"Mr. Silver," said the judge, "I been on the bench, and I got to be quite a judge of lying when I was paid a government salary. But I never heard anybody lie as fast and as hard as you!"

The smile left the face of Silver.

"You shouldn't say that," he remarked. "Nothing gives you a right to say that. I'll want an apology for that, if you please."

"Apology? Not much!" exclaimed Brender. "If you didn't use your eyes and your ears, how'd you come to know all about Rap—except you pretend that you don't know his name. Because even you know that pretending to know his name would be pretty thick! How'd you come to know these things? How'd you come to know what he looks like?"

"I saw some pictures of him when he was a boy—pictures in that album," said Silver.

"There ain't any names in there," said the judge angrily. "You couldn't tell which was him!"

"There were half a dozen pictures of one face—from four years up to twelve or fourteen," said Silver. "Only the son of the house would have as many pictures in the family album."

"Humph," said the judge. "It don't give you no idea about his inches, not out of a picture book like that."

"You're big, and his mother is small," said Silver. "I simply guessed that your boy might be of a size between the pair of you."

"Yes," said the judge, "that makes a sort of sense. But tell me how comes it that you knew he was always like something on springs, ready to jump?"

"I guessed that from the rest of his character, and by the look of his face when he was a boy."

"Character? What d'you know about his character? Who told you that he liked to shoot big game, and hold his fire till the last fool second, the way I've seen the idiot do?"

"He shot that grizzly bear—the one whose head is mounted in the hall."

"How do you know that?"

"The hair is still sleek, and has a sheen. I should say that bear was shot inside the year."

"Humph!" grunted the judge. And again he narrowed his eyes at the stranger. But this time he had a doubt. It might be that Mr. Silver was really using brains, and not merely hearsay. "I might 'a' shot that bear myself, for that matter."

"One-legged men don't go bear hunting," answered Silver. "Besides, you've been on those crutches for about two years."

"Eh? Two years? How come you put it down to that length of time? Matter of fact, I might 'a' been on them all my life!"

"You'd handle them better if you had had them that long," said Silver. "But the rubber tips are pretty well worn. So I imagine about two years is the time."

"Within a few months, you're right," admitted the judge. "But get back to the boy. You ain't said how you know that he holds his fire when he goes shooting."

"That grizzly was shot straight between the eyes. They've repaired the damage, but they couldn't help letting a bit of the fur rough up where the hole was made. And usually a man shoots a bear through the shoulder, if he gets a chance at a distance that's safe. A shot right between the eyes is careful work, or else it's done at close hand. From the character of your son, I guess at close range."

"Either," said the judge, "you heard all this before, or else you're one of the slickest pieces of thinking machines that I ever come across. But you said that he liked fast horses. How come that you guessed that?"

"I saw a pair of very neat grays galloping in that field. A man of your age doesn't care so much about showy horseflesh. Besides, your weight would break down horses of that build. They're too fine to be used for punching cattle. No cowboy could afford them. So I take it that they belong to your son. A man who owns horses like that is pretty sure to race them when he gets a chance. And a fellow who races is sure to gamble."

"By thunder," breathed the judge, "by the look of a man's shoe you could tell whether his grandfather was clean shaved or wore a beard. What made you guess at cards?"

"A fellow who gambles can't keep away from poker in

this part of the world, and a fellow like your son wouldn't play except for high stakes."

"You said he doesn't care what sort of people he's with, so long as they're exciting."

"He's gone astray, he's in disgrace," answered Silver.

"What makes you say that?"

"There," said Silver, pointing, "is where his picture used to hang on the wall."

He indicated a square patch between two windows, slightly darker than the wall paper that was around it.

"Well," declared the judge, "you got eyes *and* a brain But it might 'a' been the picture of his grandfather that hung there."

"The picture hasn't been up very long," said Silver. "Otherwise there would be more difference between the color of that paper and the paper around it. That paper has been on the wall for more than twenty years."

The judge sighed in a sort of pleasant despair.

"You pretty near beat me." he admitted. "But, far as you know, he may be dead, not disgraced at all!"

"If he were dead," said Silver, "his picture would be back on the wall."

The judge banged his crutches on the floor and then stared mutely at his guest.

"Well," he said, "I guess we'll go out and look at you on a horse. I've always said that a man would have to shoot and ride and think before I'd hire him."

He led the way, swinging clumsily along on his crutches, and, as they came out on the front veranda, he saw a great golden chestnut at the hitchrack, seventeen hands of glory.

"Hey!" exclaimed the judge. "Is that your hoss?"

"Yes," said Silver. "Come here, Parade."

It then appeared that though the great horse stood at the hitchrack, it was not tied, for it turned at once and came straight to its master's hand.

"All right! All right!" said the judge. "I'd like to know—what sort of a price did you pay for that?"

"Not a penny," answered Silver. "I caught him wild."

The judge looked for a long time at nothingness. Then he whistled softly.

"I guess we don't need to see you ride no pitching mustangs, Silver," he said. "If you want the job, you're hired."

"I don't work for hire," said Silver.

"Then what are you doing here, wasting my time?" shouted the angry judge.

"Because I'll work for nothing if the job is my sort."

"Well," snarled the judge. "I dunno what your sort may be, but what I want ain't likely to be your job. Not anywhere near."

He waved his hand toward the mountains. Brown and blue and azure, the great tide of the mountains swept raggedly away to the north and west.

"I want him home again," said the judge. "The poor lad's gone wild because I dressed him down with the rough side of my tongue a few times. His ma is breaking her heart. I'm sort of broke, too. Because up there in the mountains, where Barry Christian is like a king, is my son Raoul Brender. Rap Brender is up there, and Barry Christian has him, and if you know all the rest, you know who Barry Christian is!"

Silver stared at the mountains, but he was seeing something more than their shape. He was seeing the lengendary and awful figure of Barry Christain as that outlaw had grown upon the mind of the world. That, then, was the country of Christian. For all the West knew that the outlaw ruled like a king over the district where he had command. Silver had undone one of Christian's empires. But the evil genius of the supercriminal was so great that he had, in an incredibly short time, built up another; many of his old band had ridden hard and fast to join up again with him.

The judge was saying: "Numbers wouldn't be no good—not if an army was to march in there to get at my boy. Because an army could get lost in one or two of those ravines yonder. And besides, everybody would know where the army was going, and what it wanted. There's hardly a squatter or a trapper or a prospector up there in the hills that doesn't work for Barry Christian and get a few odd dollars out of him now and then. Those that ain't on his list hope to get there. He's like a king. He lifts his little finger and the head of a man goes off. Nobody even dares to run for a job of sheriff unless he gets the permission of Barry Christian first. But what an army can't do, one man with nerve and brains can do. Partner, what's your first name?"

"Why," said Silver, "my name doesn't matter particularly. I'm called Arizona, or Silvertip, or Silver, or Arizona Jim, or Jim Silver. You can pick out any of the lot."

He fell to plucking at his belt, unbuckling it and then drawing it up a little tighter. Still his eyes hunted through the rough wilderness of the mountains.

"And all the desert beyond, too," said the judge. "All that you can see and think of in that direction is under the thumb of Barry Christian. And still one man might beat him. Jim Silver, are you the man?"

Silver took off his sombrero and smoothed back his hair. He sighed again almost audibly. But a tenseness began to appear about his face, and his chin lifted a little.

"I don't know that I'm the man," he said. "Even if I get my hands on your son, I don't know that I'll be able to persuade him to quit the life with Christian and come back with me. Maybe I'm a fool, yet there's something inside me that tells me I'll have to try to be the man!" He did not tell the judge of his previous encounters with the man who held this part of the world in terror. But in his heart was the excitement of knowing that again he was to match wits and courage with his archenemy.

II

Crowtown

JIM SILVER had hunted for trouble; he stepped into the path of events, and then they started to overwhelm him. But all was pleasant in the beginning.

It was spring as he came across the mountains, late spring. The wind through the pass was soft. It had been blowing several days, and flowers were blooming wherever it touched. It had dissolved the finger of ice which had been laid on the lip of every cataract all through the months of winter, and now steel-blue water slid down the slopes or poured like feathery snow from the higher rocks. The pain went out of the heart of "Silvertip," also, and he began to sing as he rode. For it seemed to him that nothing was worth finding except adventure.

Now the trail grew dim. It became so steep that he dismounted to climb the rocks, while the golden stallion followed him like a dog, leaping cat-footed from one meager purchase to another. No man-trained horse could have gone safely over this way, but Parade was wild-raised and wild-caught. Even so, when his master passed out of sight among the rocks now and then, he whinnied anxiously, and Silvertip whistled in answer.

So they came to the top of the old pass and looked down to the new one that wound far below them into the ravine. There lay the little village of Crowtown, half on the floor of the valley, and half climbing one side of the gorge. Paint had never freshened it; it looked the color of dirt. Silvertip stared down at it with a casual eye, and the stallion glanced from the town, which meant sweet hay, grain, and the warmth of a barn, to his master, whose way was generally through the wilderness. Sun-beaten desert or storm-beaten mountains were usually his choice.

Silver would have turned away from the town on this occasion, also, because he felt that he had not yet penetrated far enough into the domain of Barry Christian. He wanted to get to the heart of the district before he ventured among men and tried his hand at the great task. But as he looked down the pitch of the slope, he saw a man riding a tough little mountain horse coming up the grade. Now and again the rider dismounted and led his horse up places where all the strong four legs of the mustang could hardly carry it. The mountaineer was in the saddle again and puffing from his climb before he came up to Silver. Then he threw up both hands in a gesture of astonishment.

"Arizona Jim!" he shouted at the top of his lungs.

Silver had recognized his man even at a distance. It was his business to remember faces, considering the number of armed men in this world who were constantly on the lookout for him. This was a new section for his exploration, but nevertheless he was on guard. The set of the heavy shoulders of the rider and something reckless and careless about the face made him remember the name.

"Hello, Granger," he said. "Don't fall off your horse."

Granger rode up and shook hands with him.

"But what are you doing here?" asked Granger. "There's a lot of room up here in the mountains, but there's not enough room for you and Barry Christian. This is his roost, and you can't perch on it. Don't you know that? Some of his men may spot you, and then you'd have no more chance than a Federal marshal, say. Everybody that knows about you, Jim, knows that you spend your time hunting down the crooks. You wouldn't last—why, you wouldn't last twenty-four hours down in that Crowtown yonder."

"Is that the name of it?"

"Yes."

"Well, ride down there with me, and see how long I last, Granger."

"Not me," answered Granger, screwing up his face. "I've got marching orders."

"From whom?"

"One of the higher-ups. One of Christian's lieutenants. I pinched the wrong man the other day. You see," he explained, "I'm a deputy sheriff, and I pinched one of Christian's workers last week. Got him into a lot of trouble—thought he was lying when he said that he belonged to the gang—and shipped him out into the hands of the real law and order."

He waved his arms as though to indicate that far away, beyond these mountains, there was actually a realm where law and order existed in force.

"Result is," went on Granger, "that I got marching orders. Had to pack up and leave the town—and my wife in it! That's the devil!"

"You had to ride out—and leave your wife behind you?" demanded Silver. "Do they treat you like that, Granger?"

"Well," said Granger, "I'm talking pretty freely, but the fact is that it's a good enough life, all right. Only, when they tell you to toe the mark, you have to toe the mark. If I went back down there, I might be shot out of the saddle."

"Still," said Silver, "I think I might be able to look after you. Don't you think so?"

"You?" said Granger. He eyed Silver curiously.

"What's in your head?" he asked. "Are you planning to buck Barry Christian?"

His eyes and his gesture called in the mountains to bear witness to such folly.

"I have a special job," said Silver. "And I'd like to talk

to you about things, Granger. Do you think that you'd actually be in danger if you went down there with me and sat for a couple of hours over some beer and answered questions?"

Granger stared at him, turned, looked down toward the village, and then shrugged his shoulders.

"All right," he said. "But you ought to remember that—Oh, well, I've had my marching orders, but, after all, they'll give me a little more time. I don't get a chance to talk with Jim Silver every day of the year. Come on, Jim. We'll find that beer."

"Well," said Silver, "if there's really danger for you down there in the village, perhaps we'd better talk up here? I want to know, for one thing, if Christian is in the habit of sending men off like this—making exiles of them?"

"It's only for a month or two, I suppose," said Granger. "But come along back to Crowtown, and we can talk there and have a beer. Hi! I could laugh when I think of what I know—Jim Silver here in the middle of Barry Christian's country!"

He began to laugh, in fact, as he turned his mustang and went down the slope, but though the mustang was as active as a cat, the big stallion, Parade, fairly passed it on the way down.

Like thunder Silver came, scattering stones and boulders before him, until he galloped Parade into the single street of the town.

The loafers on the veranda of the hotel stood up to see him and the horse, for the flash of Parade was more to the eyes of a Westerner than the gleam of gold. In front of that hotel they paused. Silver slid to the ground, pulled off the light bridle, and told the horse to get a drink. Water was running constantly out of a rusted iron pipe into the double trough in front of the hotel, and Parade tried it with his nose, then plunged his face in almost to the eyes.

Silver stepped aside to watch Granger tie the mustang, and a tight little crowd gathered to look the stallion over. Stockinged in black silk, with a sooty muzzle, also, the rest of him was richest chestnut. The eyes of those mountaineers went over him like loving hands and never touched a fault.

The oldest man took from his mouth a pipe whose stem had been worried short.

"Too big for mountain work," he said, measuring the seventeen hands of Parade.

"I seen him come down the west slope," said a boy with horsehide boots. "I seen him come off the old trail that mostly goats has used for years. I reckon he's a mountain hoss, all right."

"He come over the old trail," said two or three men, speaking together.

Parade had finished drinking. He lifted his head and laid back his ears, which was enough to spread out the circle of watchers. He whinnied and canted his head like a dog to hear an answer. The answer came in the form of a thin, piping whistle from inside the hotel; Silver had entered with Granger. Parade straightway went to find the master. He climbed the steps while the crowd hooted with joy. He crossed the rotten boards of the veranda with a crouching step. He was half through the doorway of the entrance when Silver appeared again.

He ordered Parade back into the street. The big stallion went. When he was off the boards at last, he showed his joy of having honest ground beneath him by frolicking like a colt up and down the street, and the size of his leaps made the weather-stained little houses look smaller still.

The crowd sifted up around Jim Silver. It was full of talk.

"Go on and have a chat with 'em, Jim," said Granger, drawing apart.

It had been warm in the sun. Silver took off his hat to enjoy the shade and the soft spring wind, and the mountaineers studied that young face and the wisdom of the quiet eyes. They marked, above all, the two spots of gray in the hair above his temples, like a pair of horns breaking through; it gave, in short, a half inhuman cast to the face. With his hat on he was a big, brown, cheerful fellow twenty-five, say. With his hat off he looked capable of anything. He was such a man that every heart in that little assemblage instantly yearned to hear the news about him. And many wistful glances were thrown at the oldest man of the village.

He, however, continued to smoke his pipe and admire the golden chestnut, but after a time he pointed the stubby stem of his pipe at the horse and said:

"That's a big un."

"Big enough for two," said Silvertip.

He produced a sack of tobacco with one hand, a pack of wheat-straw papers with the other. His ambidextrous fingers, unguided, unheeded by his eyes, built and rolled the cigarette with instant dispatch. The tip of his tongue sealed the loose lip of the cylinder; a match flared in the hollow of one hand, which mysteriously served as a windshield better than two hands would for most men. And now he was smoking, taking in generous breaths, letting thin wreaths escape while he talked.

"Prospecting, likely," suggested the old man of the village. "I've knowed gents that stayed out two year at a time prospecting."

His eyes, as he spoke, examined the long-fingered, brown hands of Silvertip, and he saw that the fingers had never been thickened and roughened by grasping the handle of a single jack or a double jack hour after hour.

"Or hunting," said the old man, "will keep a gent out a long time now and then. I recollect old Si Waltham staying away a year and a half once, and he never—"

Here a ten-year-old boy cut in with a shrill voice: "Tell us about yourself, mister! Tell us all the news!"

At this the people laughed, but they cut the laughter short in hope that an answer might come, after all.

Silvertip smiled at the lad, and his smile drew the youngster a sudden step or two closer.

"I'll tell you the whole story of my life, friends," said he. "I was born over there"—he waved to the northern horizon—"and I'm going over there"—he indicated the south and west—"and all the years in between I've been on my way."

The people chuckled. The good nature, the smile, the gentle eyes of this man delighted them, no matter how he put off their inquiries. Besides, in the West it is considered undignified for a man to talk about himself.

"Whatcha going to get when you reach yonder?" asked the boy.

"I'm going to walk right out into the horizon," said Silver, "and I'm going to dip up a bucket full of skyblue."

"Hey, and what would you do with that?" asked the boy.

"I'd sell it for paint," said Silver. "I'd come right back here to Crowtown and sell it for paint."

They were still chuckling when the tragedy happened.

Silver had seen a man ride into the head of the street on

a tough, low-built mustang, a true mountain horse. He had seen, not because there was anything particularly suspicious about the big shoulders and the shaggy beard of the rider, but because it was Silver's business and necessity to use his eyes constantly. When he was among other men he had to watch faces—and hands! He had to sit in corners, if he could, and a corner near a window was the best place of all, for sometimes he might need a quick exit.

So he saw this fellow ride down the street, jouncing a little in the saddle on account of the harsh gait of the mustang, until he was just in front of the hotel. Then he turned in the saddle with a revolver in his hand and fired.

On the edge of the veranda stood Granger, waiting for Silver to free himself from the crowd. As the shot sounded, it was Granger who threw up his arms above his head and leaned slowly backward and outward, until he pitched off the edge of the veranda and landed in the street with a loose, squashing sound, like a skin of water.

Silvertip had drawn a gun the instant the shot was fired, but he could not shoot in reply, because all the villagers had huddled suddenly between him and the assassin, as though of a common purpose to keep him from using the gun.

"Butch Lawson!" cried several voices, groaning out the words.

"He'll butcher no more men!" raged Silver, bursting through their ranks.

But "Butch" Lawson was out of sight; there was only a rattle of hoofs in the distance.

Some of the men of Crowtown started picking up the fallen body. Others stood about with clumsy, empty hands, staring at one another.

"Somebody tell Mrs. Granger," said one.

"No, don't tell her. She's poorly, anyway. Don't tell his wife."

"She's gotta be told."

"Where's Doc Wilson? I'll fetch him."

But not a soul in the assemblage made for a horse or pulled a gun, Silver noted.

A sickness of disgust rushed up from his heart into his throat. It was only owing to his safe conduct that Granger had been willing to return to Crowtown, and now he lay as if dead.

Silver ran to the golden stallion, leaped into the saddle,

and turned the horse with a cry and a touch of his knee, while he reached out and tossed the bridle over the head of Parade.

Off to the side he saw the face of Granger as the poor fellow was lifted. The head fell loosely back from the shoulders; the long hair fell back, also; the face was white; the mouth sagged open.

"Death," said Silver to himself, and raced the stallion down the street.

Except for him, Granger by this time would have been far away in the mountains, riding safely off to his temporary exile.

This thought dug like a knife between the ribs of Silver. He groaned and then drew his breath between his hard-set teeth. So he came out of town, and in view of the northwestern trail.

III

A Gold Watch

THAT trail was looped generously up a slope spotted with trees and great rocks, and mantled over with the yellow-green of new grass. The fugitive was not in view, but the noise of pounding hoofs blew back to the pursuer.

To rush up that trail was simply to invite a bullet through the brain. A man will do a second murder to escape punishment for a first, of course.

Silver did not hesitate. He aimed straight up the side of the mountain, a bit to the left of the widest loop of the trail. The stallion took him with one grand sweep up the first part of the rise; then he flung himself out of the saddle and ran on foot the rest of the way. The slope rose like a wall, but still he ran, with short, digging steps.

If he fell, he would have rolled to the bottom of the hill, so great was the downward pitch. When he ventured a glance behind him and below, he could see the village growing smaller, drawing together. He could see the hotel, where he had been a moment before, the crowd still gathering in the street, and by the white of the faces he knew that they were all looking up toward him, tracing his course of vengeance.

Off to his right the noise of hoofs rushed straight at him. The head of the stallion labored up and down beside him. And now he stepped out, with sudden grace of relief for his aching legs, onto the narrow level of the trail.

The mountain horse and the mountaineer with the ragged beard heaved into view that same instant. It seemed that the mustang knew the meaning of the leveled gun of the stranger, for it halted instantly, sliding on braced legs.

"Get down," said Silver.

The man of the beard did not move. His eyebrows were shaggy, like the beard, and the small, bright eyes glittered beneath them.

"Put your hands up over your head and get down," said Silver. "Don't take chances with this gun!"

The two hands, a little blacker than mere sunshine could stain them, began to rise. When they got breast-high, they fluttered and struggled for an instant. Then they rose above the head. The fellow turned, swung his right leg over the horn of the saddle, and slid down to the ground.

He faced Silver with the same bright, animal eyes, with a sort of beastly patience and endurance about him that was almost touching. There was a moment of silence, and in it Silvertip listened to his own breathing, and to the creaking of cinches as the sides of the great stallion heaved. Beyond these sounds he heard the windy rushing of a waterfall not far away, and a small stream was gurgling, and bubbling straight across the trail.

"Turn your back to me, Butch," said Silvertip.

"Whatcha going to do?" asked Butch.

"I'm going to fan you, and then march you back to Crowtown."

"I ain't going back," said Butch Lawson.

"You're not going back?"

Butch dropped his glance toward the leveled gun and then shook his head.

"No, I ain't going back," he said.

He wagged his head toward the town.

"They'd sort of claw me up," he said calmly.

Not one of those townsmen had joined in the pursuit, even with Silvertip to lead them, but Silver could well understand that if a helpless prisoner were brought back among them, he might be "sort of clawed up."

"You're in my hand, Butch," said he.

"Well, go ahead and close your hand," said Butch. "But I ain't going back. You shouldn't need more'n one shot to finish me, I guess."

He contemplated, with odd satisfaction, the steadiness of the gun in the hand of Silvertip. The high light on top of the barrel did not waiver.

"Why did you kill Granger?" asked Silvertip.

"Is he dead, sure enough?" asked Lawson.

"I guess he's dead enough," answered Silver.

"I'm dog-gone glad of that."

"You hated him, eh?"

"Me? Why, no. I didn't hate him."

"But you're glad he's dead?"

"Well, I'm going to die now, and nobody would wanta die for a job that he hadn't finished."

"If you didn't hate him, why did you kill him?"

"Why? Orders, you fool! What other reason would I be having?"

"Orders from whom?"

"You dunno, eh?" asked Butch.

"No," said Silvertip.

"Well, I ain't going to tell you, then."

"If you're going to die, Butch, what difference does it make if you tell the truth?"

"Because if I tell you, they'll find a way to make hell hotter for me. Besides, why should I talk to you?"

Silver stared at him. A solitaire, that loveliest songster of the West, exploded its pent-up melody from the top of a bush not far away.

"You're a good hand with a revolver, Butch?" said Silver.

"Fair to middling," said Lawson.

"So am I," remarked Silver. "I'm going to give you an even break."

He caused the gun that was in his hand to disappear under his coat. At once the hand of Lawson jerked back toward the right hip, but paused. He seemed bewildered.

"I dunno that I make it out," declared Lawson, shaking his head.

"What don't you make out?"

"Suppose that I put a slug in you, it's all right. But suppose you shoot me, it ain't going to do you no good. They'll get you afterward. They'll get you if it takes ten years and a million dollars."

"Who'll get me?"

"I've told you something, and you wanta know what. I tell you something more—haul out of here—get off my trail—clear out of the country, and maybe no more trouble'll come down on you."

"Thanks," said Silver. "Now, will you listen to me?"

"Yeah. I'll listen, I guess. For a minute. Then I'm starting."

"The next time that solitaire starts its song, we go for our guns. Does that suit you?"

"Sure," said Butch. He broke into a violent laughter suddenly, though still he kept his chin down as one prepared for instant action. "You wanna die to music. And that's all right by me."

"Are you ready?" asked Silver.

"Ready and right," said Lawson.

"Then be still, and wait for the song."

They waited. All the sounds from the valley drew suddenly in upon the ears of Silver, as though he were flying down through the air toward the ravine. Or was it simply that every sense had grown more tensely alert? Then the sweet whistle of the solitaire burst out again.

He shot Butch Lawson through the chest while Lawson's gun was still swinging up. Butch fired into the ground. A spray of gravel dashed against the knees of Silver. He saw Lawson staggering, losing balance, falling backward, and it seemed a horrible thing to let the body strike the ground.

He got to Lawson in time to catch him beneath the armpits and so lower him till he was prone.

Lawson looked straight up into the sky.

"I got enough," he said thickly. "I give up."

The red was running over his chest. Lawson put his two hands over the spot, lifted them, and the blood dripped down into his face while he looked at his crimson hands.

"Am I going to die?" asked Lawson.

"You're going to die," said Silvertip. He was a sick white. He added: "I wish that I'd never seen Crowtown!"

Then: "Lawson, nobody can help you. You're passing out fast. But if there's any message I can take for you, if there's any word you want to send—I'll take it."

"Will you?"

"Yes."

"No matter where I wanta send it?"

"Yes."

Lawson pulled out a flat gold watch; earned money could never have bought it for him.

"Gimme a knife," he directed.

Silvertip took out and opened a pocketknife. With the point of the knife, with a staggering hand, Lawson carved a scroll on the back of the gold case.

"Take it to Cooper Creek. Give it to Doc Shore," said Lawson. "He'll understand."

"Is that all?"

"That's all," said Lawson.

"No personal message that you want to send? No friend—"

"I ain't such a fool!" said Butch harshly. "What would I want of a friend—"

He began to pant, saying "Ha-ha-ha," rapidly with every outgoing breath. He opened his mouth, but could not get enough air. He began to bite at the air. He lifted himself on one elbow, and then turned on his side.

His panting turned into another sound as he tried to speak.

Silver dropped to one knee, waiting for the words.

Then the panting stopped, and Butch Lawson lay down softly, pressing his face against the ground.

IV

Copper Creek

Silvertip washed the blood from the watch at the rivulet that ran across the trail a few steps away. The water was so cold that the tips of his fingers turned pink, and an icy ache penetrated at the roots of his finger nails.

Then he mounted the stallion and rode on back to Crowtown, leaving the mustang contentedly cropping the tender young grass near its master.

When he got into the town, he found a crowd still milling about in front of the hotel and on its veranda. And everybody looked at him with wide, still eyes. When he asked questions, people answered him in low voices. They wanted to know what had happened between him and Lawson. He shook his head and asked about Granger.

"Granger ain't dead," they said. "He's lucky. He ain't dead. The bullet just run around his ribs, is all. It's a good thing Granger wasn't bumped off."

There had been no reason, then, to kill that man who now lay with his face pressed against the trail high up the hillside. There was no reason to have *"them"* on his trail. *"They"* were of course the men of Barry Christian, who would spend ten years and a million dollars to revenge Butch Lawson.

Silver made a cigarette and lighted it. His face was as calm as a stone.

"Can I see Granger?" he asked.

"Sure. Everybody is seeing him."

They took Silver into the hotel. Granger lay on a couch, propped up a little by many pillows. He was suffering pain; the lines of it were drawing deeper and deeper into his face.

His eyes glinted sidewise at Silver, and then resumed the consideration of the cracks in the ceiling. Sweat was oozing out on his forehead all the time. A woman with stooped shoulders, and a shawl over them, was on her knees beside him. She dried the sweat on her husband's face now and then and said nothing, simply watched him. Other people were in the room. They all stood back in corners, looking, listening, as though they could see the soul departing.

"Butch is lying dead on the trail yonder," said Silver.

The deputy sheriff turned his head and stared.

"They tol' me you went up after him," said he. "Did you fix him?"

"I thought he'd killed you," said Silver. "He shot you from behind. I thought he'd killed you. I went up and stopped him. He wouldn't come back. We fought it out with a clean break. Butch is dead."

He looked at the deputy sheriff, and Granger looked back at him. Other voices stirred and were silent in the corners of the room. Death, after all, had come. It seemed a satisfaction to them, in a way, to know that the alarm had not been for nothing. And this was a big day in the history of the village. Twenty such days are about all that a mountain town can count upon in the whole course of its existence.

"You want to hold me for the killing?" asked Silver.

A murmur of protest came out of the corners of the room. The deputy sheriff rolled an agonized but reproving eye, and the murmur ceased.

"Is the wound in front?" asked the deputy sheriff.

"Yes."

"Where you going to be—if we want you?"

"I'm going to Copper Creek."

The deputy sheriff blinked.

"Why Copper Creek?" he asked.

"Why not?" said Silver.

"Well, all right," said the deputy sheriff slowly. "You can go."

Silver said to the other bystanders: "I want to be alone with Granger for a couple of minutes. Will you let me have that time with him?"

No one answered. They looked at Silver and then at one another, but nobody moved.

"Get out, all of you!" said Granger.

At that they moved with shambling feet, like a flock of sheep, and trooped in one mass out of the room.

Silver said: "Granger, Christian's men are going to hunt me down, of course. Well, all that I want is a fair chance to fight back. I can't fight all of Barry Christian's gang, but I might be able to fight Christian himself. What I want you to do is to give me one steer that will help to put me on his trail."

Granger looked at him with blank, indifferent eyes.

"In the old days," said Silver suddenly, "I was useful to you once. I hate to remind you of that day. But I have to."

"I know," said Granger, "I'd 'a' got a slug of lead through me, except for you, that day in the saloon."

"Let me have a direction to follow toward the trail of Christian. That's all I ask for. Will you help me, Granger?"

"I've listened to you once before. And now I'm here with lead pumped through me," said Granger. "You go wherever you please. Go to the devil, for all of me. I won't talk to you any more."

He shut his teeth and his eyes. Silvertip stared at him for a moment, and then went from the room, stepping softly over the faded roses of the worn carpet.

When he was out in the street, he asked the way and the distance to Copper Creek. It was down on the edge of the desert, they told him. It was twenty miles away through the mountains, downhill all the way. And it was among the foothills close to the edge of the desert.

So he mounted the stallion and started at once.

He was in no haste in his preparations. Some of the men came out onto the veranda to watch him start. They said nothing. They merely looked at him with troubled eyes. When they spoke, it was very softly, to one another. And when at last he was outside of Crowtown, Silver felt as though he had left the darkness of a nightmare and come into a safely lighted room.

It was true that the twenty miles to Copper Creek were almost all downhill. Then, as he came out through a ravine, he looked down on the desert like gray mist, and saw in a lower valley the blinking windows of the town, which was stretched out long and thin through the windings of a gorge.

Copper Creek was a word that had had much meaning for Deputy Sheriff Granger. What could that meaning be? At least, there was a sinister significance attached to the place. The very mention of it had caused Granger to look on Silver as upon a lost soul.

But when he rode into the town, it looked to him like any other place which had once been a booming mining town and since then has shrunk its interests to less exciting forms of adventure. There was a line of houses at scattered intervals, or crowded shoulder to shoulder, on either side of the creek. Two-thirds of those houses were vacant. Half of the remainder had fallen into disrepair over the heads of the occupants. Because people who live in a dying town seem to take it for granted that disrepair, like disease, is catching, and hardly worth fighting against.

He passed the small district of shops. The sun was far down in the western sky, so that a rolling crimson fire walked across the windowpanes to the left of Silver. And the same light made the stallion gleam brightly enough to startle the attention of people who lounged on their front porches at the end of the day. The beauty of Parade pulled to attention a group of small lads who were scampering across the street in a game of tag.

"I'm looking for a fellow called Doc Shore," said Silver. "Can you tell me where to find him, sons?"

"Doc Shore?" they echoed in three shrill voices that melted into one phrase of sound.

And then they were silent, staring.

They knew "Doc" Shore, and they did not know him favorably. That much was clear.

"Doc Shore!" he repeated. "Where can I find him?"

The smaller lads stood silent. The eldest hooked a thumb over his shoulder.

"That way," he said.

Silver rode gloomily up the street. For he began to feel that the last request of Butch Lawson had loaded him with something more than a watch with a gold case and Swiss works. This foreboding grew on him with every step Parade made, until he saw, to his left, the little golden moons of a pawnbroker's shop, and across the window the letters: "Dr. Shore."

Silver sighed with relief. Perhaps there was, in the mind of the dying Lawson, a memory that he owed some obscure debt to Shore. For that reason he had commissioned Silver to return the watch—to its rightful owner, perhaps?

At any rate, that made a clear explanation. It was only the little scroll which Lawson had cut into the back of the gold case that troubled Silver. The thing might have a meaning more than he could understand, or it might simply have been the signature of a man unable to write his own name.

He dismounted, slapped the neck of the stallion, and, knowing that the horse would now stand there patiently, waiting for him until the ground took fire beneath his feet, Silver walked into the pawnbroker's shop.

A little man with a double stream of misty beard hanging from his chin, and pink-rimmed eyes, and a red-mouthed smile, stood up from a high stool and put the flat of both hands on the counter.

So he waited, still smiling, still expectant. The white hairs of the beard were so sparse that they did not hide the features beneath it.

Silver slid the watch onto the counter; he kept his hand over it.

"You know Butch Lawson?" he asked.

The little old man kept on smiling, but his eyes rolled upward in the act of memory.

"Butch Lawson?" he repeated.

He continued to reflect. Then his pale eyes focused with a sudden brightness on the face of Silver.

"Are you a friend of his?" he asked.

"Do you know him?" countered Silver.

"Oh, very well!" said Doc Shore. "Of course I know Butch. But sometimes the names of a few of the boys pass out of my memory. One cannot remember everything, you know. The mind balks at too many details—and I'm an old man! But Butch is a friend of yours?"

"Butch is dead," said Silver.

If there were friendship between them, it would be a shock to the pawnbroker, but Silver felt that a shock was due to the oily flow of the old man's talk.

The pawnbroker accepted the news with a mere lifting of his brows.

"Dead, eh? Tut, tut! Well, young men may die before the old ones. So poor Butch is dead?"

"And he asked me to take this to you. He asked me while he was dying," said Silver.

He uncovered the watch.

The pawnbroker lifted it, weighed it, looked at Silver with surprised eyes, and then turned the watch on its face.

What he saw on the back made him duck his head down suddenly.

Then slowly he straightened. The smile was gone from his red lips. They puckered a little, and the thin mist of the beard spread out thinner than ever, from side to side.

"Well, then," said the pawnbroker, "I'm glad to have the watch. I thought that Butch might have forgotten me. But honesty will show its hand when a man dies. And there we are!"

He spread his hands on the counter again, and the smile came back to him.

"You're staying in Copper Creek a while?"

"I'm leaving in the morning," said Silvertip. "So long and good luck to you!"

He stepped out of the door. As it closed, a bell jingled softly, and, glancing back, he saw that the pawnbroker still leaned over the counter, staring fixedly before him. There was no longer a smile, but a look of such evil as Silver never had seen on a human face.

V

The Warning

Silver went to the hotel, booked a room, and sat for a time on his bed, staring out the window. In its narrow frame were held an immensity of mountains, like great thoughts in the span of a brow. The distances turned from blue to purple, to dusty black, and the night walked up to the window and breathed through it. But still Silver remained there, thinking. His old wounds touched him with fingers of pain; he felt a weakness, a running out of strength, a breathlessness.

So he stood up suddenly. He knew that it was fear that had come into him like the cold, damp breath of a cellar, and the way to get out of it was to move into some sort of action. The nightmare in his mind was persisting. He kept seeing the dead man, Lawson, sit up on the trail, and then rise, and walk to him with dead eyes, and laughter behind that ragged beard.

Christian, like the devil in other lands, was here the root of all evil. And Silver walked in a mist.

He thought of the dead man; he thought of the evil face of Doc Shore.

Silver went down to the street and into a restaurant that had a lunch counter built in front of the stove, and some little tables scattered through a long and narrow room. Silver usually took a corner table, but he was too preoccupied to care where he sat just now, so he picked out a place halfway down the wall and slid into a chair.

The waiter came out to him in a white apron spotted with grease, and began to arrange the salt and pepper shakers aimlessly while he waited for the order.

"Friend of Doc Shore's?" he asked with an elaborate nonchalance.

Silver looked at a blunt bulldog face with the hair brushed stiffly up in a high pompadour. He looked down at the black and broken nails of the waiter's hands.

Then, with irritation, he demanded: "When a man asks for a pawnbroker, does it prove that he's the pawnbroker's friend?"

The waiter started a little. He made gestures with both hands as he answered:

"Oh, sure it don't. It don't prove nothing at all!"

But it was plain that the fellow thought it proved a great deal. His eyes squinted, and he smiled a bit to one side of his face, as though he were able to speak important things if he cared to do so. It was the attitude of the man who will demonstrate that his wits are as good as the next fellow's.

Silver ordered a steak with fried potatoes and onions, and mashed turnips, and a wedge of apple pie, and coffee with hot milk. He was still waiting for the order when a slender youth of two and twenty, with a dark and handsome face, came smiling into the restaurant and straight past Silvertip toward the lunch counter. His lips did not seem to part, and yet Silver distinctly heard words in the air as the stranger went by. And the words were: "Leave Copper Creek—fast!"

Silver drew a breath, and with that breath came the urge to leave Copper Creek, and Crowtown, and that whole section of the range, and never return to it. What we fear most of all is what we cannot understand, and Silvertip could not understand.

He should get up from his table, cancel his order, and march from the restaurant, saddle Parade, and take his pack from the hotel, to fade from Copper Creek into the outer night. That was what the advice of the stranger had been, obviously; that was what his own instincts told him to do. But a strange thing held him.

He could not tell why the dark and handsome face of the man seemed so familiar to him, but he could almost touch it with his memory, almost give it a name—though at the same time something told him that he never had seen those features before.

Then he suddenly remembered the pictures in the old album in the house of the judge. He remembered the photograph of the fourteen-year-old boy, and his mind shut like a trap on the truth. This was Raoul Brender, nicknamed "Rap." This was the goal of his search!

And "the goal" had murmured the warning to leave at once!

Suddenly Jim Silver was afraid.

He began to ask himself if the nerve which had always been his was abandoning him at last—if courage is like cloth, a thing that can be rubbed through and worn out? He had heard that in a good many places, and more than once he had had frightful chances to see men of reputed bravery show yellow—yes, and in front of a crowd. Perhaps the same thing was happening to him. Perhaps the last act of grim courage in his life had been the interception of Butch Lawson, and the execution of that man.

Execution was a better term, Silver felt. It had not been murder; it could not even be called a killing; it was simply that society had been outraged, and that Silver had been society's tool to put the matter of the outrage right.

So he remained there. He heard the cook break out into hearty laughter, and bawl:

"Rap Brender, you're a card, all right!"

And Rap Brender laughed, also. He had given a warning to a stranger, and now he sat at the lunch counter, laughing and chatting. There was little care on the mind of this Rap Brender, but Silver would have given a great deal to know what was in Rap's mind. Somehow, he felt, there was a way of linking everything together—Crowtown, Lawson, Deputy Sheriff Granger, the gold watch, the mark that had been cut on the back of the watch—a sort of double L turned downward—and finally old Doc Shore.

Looking back into his memory, Silver could swear that the last expression of Shore had been that of one ready to do murder. And therefore murder was now in the air. It was not for the sake of some small thing that Brender had warned him, but because his very life was endangered.

In our dreams, our thoughts will summon up before the closed eyes of the mind the faces we name. So it seemed to Silver now, as he thought of Shore and looked vacantly toward the big window that fronted on the street. For there the face of the pawnbroker took shape—the divided mist of white beard, the red, smiling mouth, and the peering eyes. Those eyes assuredly found Jim Silver, dwelt upon him for a moment, and then Doc Shore broke into laughter as he turned away.

Jim Silver felt that sinister mirth in his very soul. It was as though Shore were so sure Silver was trapped and so familiar with the game that he did not even care to pause to see the finish of the quarry.

The food came in a long, oval platter nicked brown at the edges. The fried potatoes sent up a rank odor of old pork fat; the onions were underdone; the coffee was acrid with chicory. And anger bubbled suddenly in the breast of Silver. He could recognize the sort of treatment that restaurant owners give to patrons they don't wish to serve. In the back of the room, the cook and Brender were laughing again, and it seemed to Silver that the laughter was a mockery directed at him.

A bow-legged cow-puncher came in. He took off a pair of ragged old leather chaps, time and sweat-blackened, and spotted with white where thorns had freshly torn the surface. The chaps he hung on a peg, looked at them, seemed to find them too grotesque dangling on the wall, and flopped them over the back of a chair. He sat at the corner table in the front of the room, facing Silver, and began to rub the tips of his fingers over the rough of his unshaven beard while he waited to give an order.

But as he gradually turned his head back and forth, one spark came out from his eyes and went into the soul of Silver. And suddenly the whole room stood up in a blaze

of light for Silver. He saw everything with a re-doubled
clearness, for he knew that if there were a danger pointing
at his life, the fellow in the corner was the weapon which
was pointing at his head.

There was only that first look, and then the man folded
his arms on the edge of the table and seemed to stare
down at his own reflections. He had a low forehead with
the flesh puckered in waves upon it; the top of his head
was like that of an infant, but the whole lower part of his
face spread out, and the nostrils flared into fish-hook twists
at the corners.

He meant business, that fellow.

Silvertip went on eating. And suddenly the onions
seemed delicious, and the steak was tender, and the coffee
was as perfect as if he had been hungering and thirsting
for a month in hard country. For the danger that had
turned him cold in prospect was merely a piquant sauce,
now that he was seeing the actual semblance of it.

Then a tall man came in, one with buck teeth that kept
him smiling, and a great knob of an Adam's apple moving
up and down in his throat. He took a chair to the side of
Silver, and, with his back against the wall, faced him in
turn. Immediately behind him entered a third, one of those
"average" men who are hard to describe, except that he
had a way of looking fixedly, taking up one thing at a
time with his eyes. He went straight down toward the rear
of the room, and seated himself at a table directly behind
that of Silvertip.

The thing was obvious now. It could hardly have been
an ordinary custom for the men of Copper Creek to sit at
the tables; the lunch counter, where the cookery could be
watched, was the natural place for hungry people to sit,
and though weariness and an abstraction of the mind had
made Silver take a table, it was hardly likely that three
other men, immediately after him, should do the same
thing. It was not chance, either, that had distributed them
in such a pattern, making Silver the exact center of the
design. The meaning was simple: he was about to be filled
with lead.

He hunched back his chair, turned slowly, and called
for another cup of coffee. The waiter came to get his cup.
That waiter was very pale now.

He snatched up the saucer and cup as though he were

removing it from before a leper. He was sweating, and not with the heat of the room.

Now that the chair had been pushed back, Silver's plan was simple. He would drop a spoon, lean for it, and slide suddenly to the floor with a gun in each hand. The fellow behind him, with the lingering eyes, must be his first target, then the man with the buck teeth, and last the cowpuncher in the front of the room. Every shot would have to tell; there could be no misses. Three snap-shots, while he lay on the floor, and every one a bull's-eye; that was the program that lay before him.

He decided that he would wait until the second cup was brought to him.

"Rap," said the voice of the man behind him.

"Yes, Larry," said Brender.

"Get the cook and the waiter out of the way," came the sudden command.

And Silver knew that he had waited too long. The thing was about to begin now.

He turned slowly in his chair, his right arm over the back of it. His position looked helpless enough, his legs crossed, his arm at that angle. But he could get his guns from under his armpits with one flashing gesture, and a thrust of his foot would hurl the table from in front of him and cast him in a backward dive toward the floor.

That moment of confusion might give him a chance to make his guns start chattering, and if that were possible, he would still have a fighting chance. But as he turned and saw the cook and the waiter slinking with frightened faces out of the little kitchen through a rear door, he estimated those chances as one in a thousand. For these were men who lived by the gun, all of them.

"If you make a fast move," said the man called Larry, "it will take you right into hell, Silvertip. Understand?"

"I understand," said Silver. "Are you the messenger boy of Doc Shore? Come here to collect me?"

"Cool, ain't he?" commented the man in the front of the room. He drew, without haste, a long-barreled Colt, and laid it on the table in front of him.

"He's cool," said the buck-toothed man at the side of the room. "He's a good ticket, and he's going to be punched for a long ride. Silver, you don't have to talk, but I'd like to know what happened to Butch Lawson."

"The slug hit him under the heart," said Silvertip. "He lasted long enough to speak a few words. That was all. Then he turned over and went to sleep."

"He lasted long enough to make a sucker out of you," remarked Larry.

"I don't know," said Rap Brender, leaning both his elbows against the edge of the lunch counter. "Maybe there was room for Silvertip to have a little surprise. I'm not so sure that he's been a sucker."

"We haven't got all night," said Larry. "Silver, you've done a few things in the world. You've built yourself a name. It's a pity that you've got to go out like this. But orders are orders. Boys, get him covered!"

"Wait a minute!" called a harsh, stern voice. It came from Rap Brender. He stood as before, but now there was a gun in each hand. "Keep your guns out of sight, partners," he was commanding. "I've got something to say to you."

"Hold on, Rap," muttered Larry. "You know where you stand already. If you butt into this game, you'll wish you were dead long before you're planted underground!"

"I hear you talk," said Rap Brender. "What I say is that Silvertip is facing the music in a way that I like to see. We're not going to jump him in a pack. We're going to take him on one by one."

It seemed to Silver that Brender grew larger, taller, as he spoke. The meaning in his face was clear, and so was the ring of his voice. It compelled a moment of silence from the others.

"Thanks, Brender," said Silver, and waited.

No matter how the thing turned out, Silver was glad now that he had come into the mountains to find young Rap Brender. The game was hard, and the chances were long, but the reward would be worth fighting for. He looked at the clean features of Brender, now drawn tense and hard, and saw that there was the true steel in him.

The buck-toothed man stood up, little by little unfolding the great length of his body.

"You been reading books again, Rap," said he. "You been reading books and getting romantic. You're going to stand by and watch three duels, are you? Why, you poor fool, this ain't what you think. This is Silver, and his guns speak a coupla dozen languages."

"Brender," said Larry, "if you don't like this job, step out the back way, and we'll finish it without you."

"I've made my talk," said Brender. "And I've made my suggestion. If it doesn't sound to you, get out of the place, the three of you. Watch your hand, Stew!"

The last was a shout. He of the fleshy forehead, in the front of the room, had snatched toward his gun, but his hand remained still in mid-air, and the gun on the table was untouched.

"You nearly collected it on the button just then," said Brender.

"I guess you know what this means, Rap," said Larry.

He stood up in turn.

Brender had a spot of white in the middle of each cheek. His dark eyes glittered.

"I know what it means," he said. "It means that I'm through. And thank Heaven for that. I always thought you were a filthy lot. Now I know it. I hoped that *you* would have clean hands, Larry, but I see you're in with the rest. Get out of this. You can go the back way."

Larry looked deliberately around the room. Then he made a vague gesture of salute to Silver.

"It looks as though you're going to win this hand, Silver," he said. "I thought we had you cooked, but you had an ace up your sleeve. Come on, boys."

He turned toward the stricken, desperate face of Brender.

"I'll be seeing you, Rap," he said, and passed on.

They moved in single file, slowly, through the kitchen and out the rear door of the restaurant. Brender and Silver remained alone.

VI

Flaming Guns

FOR an instant the world receded from them, and in the moment of silence, staring at one another, each realized what he had found in the other.

"Are you coming with me or riding alone?" asked Silver.

"With you," said Rap Brender. "My horse is in the hotel stable with yours. But Christian's men may have the stable guarded by this time. We've got to run like the devil. Come on!"

They went out of the restaurant with a rush. The thunder of their footfalls was still echoing through the long wooden box of a room when they stepped into the dust of the street. Ahead of them two forms, bending far forward, were sprinting across the way and into the dark throat of an alley, as Brender and Silver headed for the hotel, with Rap well in the lead.

And as he ran, Silver saw the image of Christian, and marveled at the genius of the man who knew so well how to gather about him men who feared nothing except himself. Shore must be one of them. The scrawl on the back of the watch must have been short for the message, "Kill the bearer."

Rap Brender glanced impatiently back over his shoulder. And, throwing off all thought, Silver was instantly up with the smaller man. But size did not matter. If it were Christian that Brender had defied for the sake of a stranger, there was the soul of a giant in this slender fellow.

He heard Brender gasping: "Take rear stable door. I'll take front!"

So they split apart, rounding to the rear of the hotel, and Silver cut back to the farther end of the long, low

42

barn. The door was open. Something moved in the tar-black interior, a shadow within the shadow, and a dull gleam of metal.

"Hold up! Who's there?" demanded a voice.

"Saddle up!" panted Silver, checking his run, but striding straight forward. "Brender's gone wrong and bolted. Saddle up and come along!"

"Brender couldn't go wrong. Who are you?"

"You fool!" said Silver.

"Back up, brother, till I know you," commanded the shadow in the broad doorway.

But the gleam of the gun had dropped from breast-high as low as the hip, and Silver took his chance.

Everything was obscurity, except the tarnished gleam of the gun and the pale spot of the face against that velvet blackness. It was guesswork to find the chin, but the fighting instinct helped him. He felt his knuckles bite home against the jawbone.

The gun flashed. The boom of it rolled through the barn, and a dozen horses sprang to their feet, snorting.

Silver already had laid the barrel of his Colt along the head of that staggering form in the darkness. The man fell under the very feet of the horses. Silver took him by the heels and jerked him against the wall.

A swift form came at him out of the darkness, calling softly: "Silver!"

"All right. He's down," said Silver, and made for Parade.

There is an extra sense that teaches a cow-puncher how to saddle swiftly in the dark. He gets his practice in the early gloom of autumn and winter mornings. Now saddle and bridle were whipped over the stallion.

"The back way! Quick!" called Rap Brender, whose hands seemed to possess a faster touch than even those of Silver.

Lantern light came pitching and swaying toward the front door of the barn. A man was shouting as he ran:

"Who's there? What's up? Jerry—Pete—come on!"

At the door of the barn, the lantern light, steadied while the bearer waited, perhaps, for the reënforcement that Pete and Jerry would bring him. But Silver was already through the rear door on Parade. And the slender form of Rap Brender was whipping into the saddle.

Off to the right, not fifty yards, two horsemen rushed

them at the run. Brender and Silver already had their
mounts under way. The wind of the gallop began to whip
Silver's face. Guns crackled rapidly. Those fellows were
fanning their revolvers or they could not have shot so fast.
Turning in the saddle, he gave them their answer, a
smooth-flowing salvo as fast as his thumb could flick the
hammer of his gun.

Five shots and a yell answered those bullets. He saw the
two pursuers split apart; darkness dissolved them as they
slowed down, and out across the open fields behind Copper Creek, Silver and Brender cut down into the narrows
of the canyon.

The ragged face of the cliff rushed by them on one side,
the broken gleaming of the creek on the other.

Brender led by a little, then by more. And Silver called
on Parade. There was the usual magnificent response. He
drew near Brender, and there he hung, with the tail of the
other horse snapping straight out, almost in his face.

Amazement came over Silvertip. He felt that he was
matched or overmatched by the generous, great heart of
Brender, but it was a prodigy that Parade should be
matched, also!

They shot out of the widening mouth of the valley onto
the wavering flat of the desert, and a warm wind blew on
them. No sound of pursuit echoed through the ravine behind them, yet Brender was jockeying his horse forward,
riding as if in a race.

Suddenly Silver understood. It *was* a race, and with all
the dangers of the present or of the future forgotten, this
light-hearted fellow was lost in the contest of horse with
horse. Once more Silver leaned forward, edging his weight
toward the withers, and this time Parade drew slowly level
with the other; then, with a sudden rush, he went away,
for the smaller horse was stopping with exhaustion.

Silver drew up to a trot, to a walk; Brender rode beside
him, shouting out in bewilderment:

"You beat Chinook! Great thunder, Silver, your horse
beat Chinook! She's beaten, and it's the first time!"

"She's a grand mare," said Silver. "She's the fastest that
ever ran against Parade—except one."

"Except what one?" exclaimed Brender.

"His old father—Brandy. Old Brandy can still hold
even or beat him for a mile or so. But Parade doesn't get
tired. That's where he wins."

"If I'd known there was a horse that could move away from Chinook like this—" groaned Brender, and paused.

"Nothing else will be apt to catch her," said Silver.

"I'd still be back home at the old man's shoulder; running the ranch," said Brender. "But she's what took me away. I watched her grow up. When she was a yearling, she could leave the bunch when they ran for water or came in from the field to the corral. I spotted her for mine. I gentled her. I broke her. And when I rode her, Silver, it seemed to me that there was nothing in the world that I couldn't catch, and that nothing could catch me. That's what started me. I was a fool. She made me feel safe. And I went to the devil at a touch. Christian didn't have to persuade me. Chinook had done the persuading already. You know. The fine, brave, free life—and no work—and all the men heroes, and all the women beautiful, and all the liquor old, and nothing but hard riding, and excitement, and—oh, you know what I mean! I rode right into hell on Chinook's back. But there's not a gamer, truer horse in the world, Silver."

It seemed to Silvertip that the whole soul of the youth had, somehow, spilled out in this one speech. There was the picture of his past, of his nature, of his raising, and of his temptation and fall.

"No," went on Brender thoughtfully, "you wouldn't even understand. You live the free life, all right. But people know that you've never been crooked. *I've* been crooked, Silver. I know what it means to stick a gun under the nose of a man. I'll tell you another thing—I've enjoyed doing it. I've liked it, and getting into brawls, and having a fight right out to the finish. *I've* been nearly finished a couple of times. But I've liked the life a whole lot."

He looked suddenly behind him, swinging half around in the saddle.

"I understand," said Silver.

"I like this, too," said Brender. "I know that they're going to get me. Christian never fails. Sooner or later the men he marks off are dead. And it doesn't take very long. But in spite of that, I sort of like this—being done with the dirty part of the old life, you know. And riding out here toward we don't know what, riding over the rim of the world—you know what I mean. And you along with me! Silver, you're a man—I don't mean just batting that fellow over the head in the barn, and I don't mean simply shooting one of that other pair out of the saddle, but I *do* mean the way you sat there in the restaurant, and waited for the music to start!"

"Rap," said Silver, "I don't want to talk about myself. What's important is the thing you've done. I was as dead as a fish out of water. And you put me back in the swim. You say that you're sure that Christian will get you. But suppose that the two of us stick together? Two men that work together and fight for one another could stand off the devil himself."

"We could beat the devil—but not Christian," said Brender.

VII

A Cry in the Night

A MOON came up, yellow like a winter sun in the far North. By the wan light of it they rode on, until Chinook was stumbling with weariness, and all of that time the high spirits of Rap Brender failed to cool. He laughed, he sang, he whistled, he rattled off cheerful anecdotes in endless succession, but he refused consistently to tell Silver what Silver most wanted to know—the ways and the habits and the numbers of the Christian gang.

He would exclaim, in answer to the questions: "Tomorrow we'll talk over everything. To-night I want to forget."

But he could plan the great party which they would indulge in before catastrophe overtook them. He laid the scene of it all the way from Mexico City to Denver, and named the drinks, and roasted the birds. It was only when Chinook began to give out that they halted.

The desert was as flat as the palm of a hand. Cactus growths stood up like men or crouched like beasts all around them, and a hunting party would not have to be as cunning as wild Indians in order to use such cover in stalking the quarry. Therefore, while Rap Brender slept three hours, Silver stood on guard walking around and around the camp in a great circle, sometimes making a halt in order to scan all the environs of the camp, and sometimes lying down so that with his ear to the ground he could hear every vibration. He made such a business of this standing watch that sleepiness did not trouble him. He allowed not one instant for his own thoughts, except for a moment when he stood close to Brender, just before waking him up.

However gay Rap had been before twisting himself into his blanket, he suffered now in his sleep, his forehead clouding, his head twisting over against his shoulder, as though forced by the hangman's knot. Then it seemed to Silver that this was a life foredoomed to waste. It was no more than a glass of liquid held in a trembling hand. It would be flung away. Perhaps already young Brender had come many times with an inch of death. He would try danger once more, and that time would be the last. He had outraged the law; now he had defied the outlaws. He was more perfectly isolated than any man that Silver could conceive of.

For all of that picture which rolled suddenly and sadly into his mind, Silver determined to stand with him, shoulder to shoulder, through every crisis.

He roused him with a word. That hair-trigger nature responded instantly, as a fine gun responds to a touch. He was out of his blanket and up, and looking around him with cool, calm eyes.

"Seen anything?" he asked.

"Nothing," said Silver. "How'd you sleep?"

"Like a top. Dreamed that I was in a castle on the edge of the world, sitting at a silver table, and eating off a golden plate. Turn in, Silver."

Silver turned in, smiling at Rap's account of his visions. He could remember the tortured face and the head pressed over on one shoulder.

Then, with one twist of the blanket around him, Silver turned his own face from the moon and went to sleep.

And, just as he had looked down at the handsome, sharply defined face of Brender, so Rap Brender now looked down on him, and saw the jaw gripped harder in sleep, and the fine shadows of resolution form in the center of the brow.

Then, with a sigh, Brender stepped back and began his

circling of the camp, his lookout for any sign of life. An owl passed like a dark gesture, shooting over his head in its hunt for mice or some other little warm-blooded life that might have ventured out in the moonlight. But there was absolutely no sign of horsemen moving across the flats, far or near.

Brender sat down cross-legged. He pulled out a pencil and a small notebook, in which he scribbled:

DEAR SILVER: I'm leaving you. I'm going to lose myself in a way you won't be able to follow.

I know that you'll try to find my trail. You feel under an obligation because I kept the thugs from murdering you, and now that I'm outside the law and the Christian gang, both, you'll want to back me up against the world.

But that's no go, Silver. If you cut loose from me, you can win through, maybe. You may be able to keep away from Christian because the law isn't hunting you. But if you stay with me, you'll surely be snagged. That's why I'm cutting off by myself. I'm leaving now and taking the chance that even Christian's bloodhounds won't be able to follow our trail by moonlight.

If you think that you're under any obligation to me, you're wrong. It was simply a lucky thing for me that you happened along to-day. Otherwise I might still be with the Christian outfit of man-killers and crooks. Whatever else the world may have against me, it can't call me a murderer, and if I had stood by while those fellows were shooting you up, murder would have been the charge against me. The moment I came into the restaurant and saw you, I knew that I didn't want to go through with the dirty job. And when I watched you face the three of them, I knew I'd have to fight on your side.

You can see that you don't owe me a thing. I owe you the chance that made me be white for once.

Don't try to follow my trail. You couldn't do me any good and you'd simply get yourself into trouble too deep for even Silver to wade through. Leave the Christian gang to itself. Nobody can beat that crowd. Not while the brains of Christian are running it. If I were you, I'd slide out of this country and go to South America until the Christian outfit has had a chance to cool off.

I would have told you all about the workings of the gang, but I knew that if I gave you a lot of information you never would have stopped until you'd tried to break up that machine. And believe me, nobody is going to be able to smash that outfit.

Meeting you was a great thing. Of course I'd heard a lot about you, but meeting you was a lot bigger and better than anything I had heard.

The best of every luck to you.

RAP BRENDER.

When he had finished writing this, he tore the pages out of the book, taking care that he made no loud sound in the ripping. Then he picked up saddle and bridle, muffling the iron of the bridle with his hand, and carried his outfit a full hundred yards from the camp.

Chinook was up and grazing, though Parade was still lying down. He led the mare to the saddle, pulled it over her back, and in another moment was leading her away.

He went on for a full quarter of a mile before he ventured to mount, in fear lest the wolf-sharp ears of Silver might hear the squeak of the saddle leather. Then he rode steadily on, keeping the line that he had held to since they left Copper Creek side by side. He maintained the direction while the moon began to climb to the zenith, but as the dawn began he altered his course.

He had entered a district of lava flow before he changed his direction. All around him the ground was covered with glass-hard slag, or cinders crumbling slowly to dust, or heaps of fragments like great black shocks of hay.

He kept to places where the black slag extended like ice, and where the hardest stampings of the mare would make little or no impression. Still clinging to that sort of going, he managed to snake his way through the miles of the lava flow and come out into the desert on the other side with the surety that Silver would not be able to stick to his trail.

That surety made him half melancholy and half gay. He felt that it was his duty to shake off Silver; but he felt, also, that it was the greatest loss in his life. And now he wanted forgetfulness at any price.

The sun was well up. The heat of the day had commenced to burn him, and he kept Chinook to a slow dog-trot that gradually drifted the miles behind them. He knew the way he wanted to keep, but he had to change direction

twice in order to get to two water holes. It was the very
end of the afternoon before he came in sight of what he
wanted. He was then facing due west, and against the red
blaze of the horizon fires he saw tall trees etched, and the
sharp wedges of several roofs. It was well after sunset before that black series of silhouettes turned into green under his eyes, a dusky green overdrawn with night shadows.

But this was the place he wanted. Chinook, with the
smell of green grass in her nostrils, lifted her dainty head
and went eagerly forward. And so they passed into the
oasis.

There was no other name for it. Thirty years before,
Tom Higgins, in his youth, had fled across the desert and
found three trees growing close beside a little spring that
bubbled up in the sand, ran a pace or two, and was drunk
up by the desert.

To Tom Higgins, half dead with thirst, the crystal shin-
ning of that water was the most beautiful thing in the
world. So he filed on the half section that contained the
spring, and went back to live there. In his equipment were
tools for digging, some seed grain, and a few tough little
saplings, a foot high, which he had dug up, roots and all,
packed in moss, and brought with him. He began to en-
large the vent of the spring. For a year, off and on, he dug
down and down until he had drilled through the bed rock,
and then he was rewarded by a thousandfold welling of
the water. It would not rise above the surface, but it made
a great source of supply that was more than sufficient for
his three or four hundred acres.

So he settled down there permanently. By degrees he
planted trees in lines and in groves. He established well-
leveled fields of alfalfa, of oats, of wheat. He made a
truck garden. He fed all his hay and grain to pigs, horses,
cattle, sheep, and once a year herded the drove across the
desert to the nearest market. He could employ servants
now, and with their help he turned his entire oasis into a
garden.

He took out a hotel license, and Higgins's hotel and bar
became a famous legend. Not many men ever got to it,
because the way was across bitter leagues of desert, but
those who finally achieved the place by design or accident,
always felt that their trip had been worth while.

Brender, coming in, first heard the lowing of the cattle,
and as he drew toward the center of the oasis, he heard

also the clank and whirring of the windmills which by day and night used every breeze to pump out of the source the life-giving water for the soil. He came through a great grove of round-headed trees into a second view of the hotel of Tom Higgins.

It was backed by sharp-roofed barns, but the house itself was in the Spanish style, and built of bed rock that had been blasted free and roughed into shape by Mexican stone cutters. A tide of green climbing vines swept up over it, and even over the four stories of the tower which Tom Higgins had built, and on top of which, men said, he took his stand every day at noon, to scan the horizon with a strong glass, as though he were a sailor once more, and on the bridge to find the position of a ship.

One thing was certain: there was that in the past of Higgins which made him expect, some day, a very important visitor. His expectation was so great that he constantly had about him a troop of the most experienced cutthroats. Their value as farm laborers was not great, but their skill with weapons was well known, and if Tom Higgins had been a sailor in his youth, now he lived like a sort of land pirate, accumulating a more and more unsavory reputation.

It mattered little to young Rap Brender that there were strange things in the air of the place. What was important to him was that there were green things to look upon, good liquor to drink, and perhaps one day of respite before Barry Christian and his gang swept over him like a black wave.

He rode into the patio, where a big man was lighting the three lanterns that illuminated the court. He had a silhouette like the shadow of an egg, for his hips and stomach were enormous, and he sloped above the waist to a comparatively narrow pair of shoulders, a vast pyramid of a neck, and a wonderfully small head which was as bald as glass.

That was Tom Higgins.

He wore a pair of old overalls, some Mexican huarachos to cool his feet, and a flannel undershirt whose sleeves had been cut off at the shoulders.

He turned to Brender a face puffed and reddened by whisky bloat, and waved a hand of greeting.

At his shout, a spindling boy of sixteen came slowly out

and took the mare, after Brender had stripped the pack from behind the saddle.

"You come in here," shouted Tom Higgins. "I ain't seen you for two years, Rap. We're going to have a drink, and I know what the drink's going to be. We're going to have some eighteen-year-old rye that's been cooking in a barrel for all of that time, and if it ain't a hundred and fifty proof, I'm a sucker."

Brender thanked him, but said he needed sleep. Three hours of sleep and he would be on deck again, but now he was too tired to enjoy even good liquor.

He sat with Tom Higgins in the big, empty dining room, and ate roast kid and baked potatoes. Then Higgins, in person, conducted him to a bedroom that faced away from the patio, and looked out upon green alfalfa fields to the east. Brender struck the bed without so much as pulling off his boots. He was asleep before the springs had stopped creaking.

When he wakened, the white hand of the moonlight lay on the floor beside the bed, and in his ears a woman's scream was still ringing.

VIII

The Girl

He listened in incredulous silence for another moment, half expecting the sound to be repeated. It was not a cry of pain, but one of fear. It came from a young throat, for there had been music in the treble of even that shriek.

Then he flashed to the door, turned the knob, and found it stuck. He tried it with hand and shoulder, and heard the bolt clank back and forth in its slot. He had been locked in!

He dropped to one knee, with a gun in his hand instinctively. Something was happening from the sight of which he was to be barred. It must be a matter of great importance, for Tom Higgins well knew that his guest had been with Barry Christian, had been one of his gang, and Tom could hardly know so soon that there had been a breach between Rap and the great chief. Or had Christian, with his usual uncanny prescience, guessed the resort to which Rap Brender would flee? Had a swift rider come across the desert, and was Brender now caught in an easy trap?

He ran to the window. There was a two-story drop, but a drainage pipe ran not far away. He was over the window sill instantly, and slithering down the pipe to the ground.

Once there, he breathed more easily; his heart stopped racing; his brain began to function like a useful engine.

The sound he had heard in his sleep might have come from any direction. In fact, it seemed to him that it must have floated into the room from a place directly outside the window. But nothing lived in the moonlight before him. Only the alfalfa extended pale and gleaming, as though covered with frost. A warm wind was blowing. It carried to him the alkaline breath of the desert beyond the oasis, and the thought, once more, of Barry Christian. A picture rushed into his mind of the many riders, and the many loping horses, swinging steadily forward on the blood trail.

He had only perhaps this single night to live through, and yet he was squandering his time on the scream of a woman!

But he turned the corner of the hotel and reached the patio entrance. The gate had been closed. He climbed, using the heavy iron bars that reënforced the wood, until he was at the top of the gate, and off that onto the top of the wall.

There he lay out on his stomach, his head pillowed in his folded arms, and looked about him. The patio of a Spanish-built house is like the brain of a man. Everything that happens in the house will sooner or later show some trace of its occurrence in the patio.

So he waited.

All the windows, like blind, black eyes, looked out on the patio. The silence was perfect. Then a rooster crowed, making a voice that sounded far, far away, coming from behind the oasis, yet it must have been close at hand. A moment later something came through the darkness of a room, something white that approached the window, that flashed in the shaft of the moonlight, and a girl leaned out over the sill.

In the speed of her glance, the rapid turning of her head as she swept the patio, there was desperation. She spun suddenly about. Another form had loomed behind her. Arms of darkness grappled her, and swept her into the shadows, as a great fish might catch prey on the surface and drag it instantly down into the gloomy depths.

The window, a moment later, was closed, the frame groaning against the sides. And the shudder of that sound was matched by the tremor in the body of Rap Brender.

He must do something. He must get to that room.

He had, at first, a feeling that the wise thing would be to go straight to his host and make inquiries. But he remembered the locked door of his room. He had been closed in until other events were concluded on this night, and his door could not have been fastened without the order of Higgins.

And was there anything of which Tom Higgins was incapable?

Brender scanned the farther wall of the patio, near the window which he had been watching. It was a sheer rise, but it was broken by a window in the first story. If he could climb by the aid of that window, his hands would reach the sill of the window above.

That was enough for him. What he could accomplish after getting into the room, he did not ask himself. Forethought rarely troubled him, but impulse ruled his actions.

He crawled back to the gate of the patio and climbed down its inside surface as easily as he had mounted from without. Then, skulking close to the wall, he rounded the patio until he was beneath the window he had marked.

It was not easy to climb. The lower window helped him, but as he gained the top ledge of it, he lost a handhold and slipped. The weight of his body jerked him free. Luck enabled him to land on his feet. He pitched forward on his hands, skinning the palms of them badly.

Then he stood up and huddled into a corner, wondering what noise his fall had made, and what eyes might have been watching him.

Nothing could be gained by such delays, he told himself, except to give fear a chance to enter him. So he tried the climb again, more cautiously. Some of the strength had gone out of him. The sound of his breathing seemed loud enough to arouse the entire household. But he gained a handhold on the sill of the upper window this time.

At that, such a strength of hope surged up in him that he was easily able to draw himself up into the casement. There was hardly any other name for the aperture, considering the thickness of the rock wall.

He put his face against the glass. There was nothing before him except darkness, that seemed to be whirling slowly before his eyes. He tried the window sash. It rose an inch, then stuck. He had to work it softly back and forth in order to raise it completely without making a sound, and as he worked he wondered what eyes might be watching him either from the outside or from the secure blackness within.

Once the sash was up he slipped into the room.

The air was warm there. The smell of the goat-skin rugs and coverings of chairs hung in the air, and another scent, too, high up the scale, like the thin, sweet vibration of a violin—the fragrance of a perfume!

Rap Brender, standing back against the wall, staring at the darkness with eyes which could plumb it hardly a step at a time, told himself that she was not only young, but beautiful. He could not be wrong. A true message had flashed to him through the moonlight across the width of the patio!

For when is instinct wrong?

He moved forward. His hands found a chair, a table. His eyes began to help him more. He saw the loom of a bed—but his carefully exploring hands discovered that it was not occupied.

He reached a door, found the knob, turned it, and gained nothing by the pull which he gave it.

He had come all this way to be stopped by a locked door, then! Suddenly, in disgust and in deep misgiving, he decided that he would return by the way he had come, and regain his room and try to fall asleep again.

He went to the window, but one glance at the patio, at the gate which he had climbed, made him set his teeth with a new determination. He had come too far to give up this effort without more of a battle.

He returned to the door. After all, it might be stuck, not locked. So he took hold on the knob, lifted hard, and felt the heavy frame, as he thought, give a trifle. A moment later it was swinging silently open against him!

He looked out into the hall. A lamp, with the wick turned low, hung down from the ceiling, and gave feeble rays up and down the length of the corridor. On either side of that hall there were doorways, any one of which might give entrance to the place where the girl was kept.

One of those doors now suddenly opened, letting out a full shaft of light from the interior. He had a glimpse of a big man wearing a great pair of mustaches, a tall and splendid fellow with the bearing of a general. With him stepped a smaller companion, dapper, lean, cat-footed, moving obsequiously beside him of the mustaches.

Brender had closed the door of his room. Now, hearing the voices coming, he pressed his ear close to the crack. He heard the footfalls; he heard a quiet, deep voice saying:

"Time and patience will cure all evils, even a woman!"

He heard a muttered answer, and the pair passed on, turning a corner, were gone from hearing.

Brender opened his door again and looked out.

Had they locked the door through which they had appeared?

No doubt they had, but they had left the key, brightly gleaming, in the lock. His heart leaped when he saw it, and, instantly gliding into the hall, he stepped to that other doorway and turned the key. The bolt slid back with an audible clank, and he quickly pulled the door open and stepped inside.

The girl stood at the farther end of the bedroom against the wall. But she was not alone. Confronting her, with back turned to Brender, was a stodgy man in an aggressive pose, and it was plain that the silence into which Brender had stepped was simply a tense pause in a combat of wills.

IX

The Guardian

HE had made a bit of noise in entering, and the turning of the lock had certainly been a distinct sound, yet neither the girl who faced him nor the man whose back was turned paid any more attention to him than figures in a dream. He had a chance to see the room, with its goatskin rug and the big, low bed; and, above all, to be surprised at the position of the lamp set in the casement. From that position it streamed its light straight at the man, and touched the girl with only a vague reflection which showed that her hair was dark and softly luminous, and gave a faint glow to her olive skin.

It was almost as hard to see her now as it had been across the distance of the patio, when the moonlight struck her, but Brender did not need to stand close. He had guessed at her as one surmises a garden in the dark by the fragrance of the rose, and by hope. To him she was beautiful, and the brightest sun and the passage of a score of years could never make him see anything other than beauty in that face.

"I'm glad you came back, Alonso," said the other man. "She's playing the stubborn devil again. No promises now. She won't commit herself. The first chance she gets, she'll start screeching like a wild cat to draw attention; she'll have us in jail unless we chloroform her and take her out of the country in the middle of the night."

He had not turned while speaking. Now the girl said:

"It's not Alonso. It's another one of your hired kidnapers!"

The man who confronted her at last whirled about, exclaiming:

"Who dares to—"

His words stopped with a jerk. He had seen the flashing

57

gesture with which Brender produced a gun. His own hand jumped nervously, but did not complete its motion to draw a weapon, for there was something in the way Rap Brender held the gun that made him seem the master. It was hardly higher than his hip, and tilted a little to the side. If he fired, it would be by the sense of pointing rather than by sight, and it was obvious that he would not point awry.

Now that Brender could see his man, he liked the looks of him very little. His skin was darker than mere sunburn could make it; there was the Mexican smoke in the whites of his eyes, and his cheeks puffed out in tight bags, swollen by good living. He had a short-cropped black mustache, and the only way he showed his emotion now was in the spreading and contraction of the bristling hairs as his mouth worked.

"Rosa," he said, "is this one of your tricks? Have you anything to do with this fellow? Young man, what do you want?" The Spanish came crowding off his lips.

"Rosa," said Brender.

"You want what?"

"He wants me, Uncle José," said the girl in English. "And he seems to be the sort of a fellow who gets what he wants."

She came away from the wall slowly. Brender had to fight himself to keep from looking at her; only from the corner of his eye he realized that she had flushed, and that she was smiling, and her beauty, as she came into the widening cone of the lamplight, warmed his heart to the roots.

"Unworthy and shameless girl!" groaned the man José. "I think you would go off with him in the middle of the night."

"What can I do?" said Rosa, still smiling. "He is armed, and we are helpless. Ha!" she cried out softly. "I knew there was one man to be found in the world."

"Young man," said Uncle José, "I don't know what sort of madness is working in your brain. If you're desperate for money, I can let you have some. Tell me what you want with—"

"Rosa," said Brender. He flashed one glance at her, adding: "Will you come?"

"Yes!" said the girl.

"Oh, fool!" cried José.

"Soft, soft," cautioned Brender through his teeth. "I saw

you at the window overlooking the patio, Rosa. Some one dragged you away from it. Was it this fellow?"

"It was," said she.

"And you'll go with me?"

"Do you ask me? Will a famished man drink cold spring water? Will a starving man eat? But wait—wait! The hotel is full of my uncle's men. The stables are filled with his horses. If you try to take me away—"

"Hush!" said Brender. "I know you want to go, and that's enough. Is your uncle armed?"

"Yes."

"Take every weapon on him."

She went straight to José and stood behind him. She was not smiling now. It was rather a silent laugh that kept her lips parted and her eyes shining.

José half turned to her with an exclamation.

"Look at me," said Brender. "And stand like a stone. I don't know the customs in your country. But up here a man who handles a woman the way you've done to-night gets his face bashed in with a gun. Stand fast, and think with your hands."

"José Murcio," said the girl, "meet my friend—"

"Brender," said he. "Raoul to my mother, and Rap to the rest of the world, Miss—"

"Cardigan."

She had reached her hands under the arms of José Murcio, drawn back his coat, and removed from inside it a pair of heavy guns.

"Those are the fangs," she said, "but there's still poison in him!"

"The law will take care of you, young man," said Murcio. "The law—"

"The law's wanted me for a long time," said Rap Brender.

The eyes of the girl widened and darkened as she looked at him over the shoulder of Murcio.

"But never for kidnaping," said Brender. "This will be something new. And I like a change of air and a change of work. Señor Murcio, back into that corner, and turn your face to the wall."

Murcio slowly retreated. He began to breathe hard, and his knees sagged.

"What are you going to do to me?" he asked.

"Look at him!" said the girl. "And with *men* he's a coward, too! Oh, Uncle José, what a king of rats you are!"

"The law," gasped Murcio. "Decency—the law—every worthy person—Treacherous devil, you have lured him here to trap me—your guardian. The wasted years I've poured out in the care of you that—"

"My wasted money that you've appropriated," said the girl with a savage outburst. "The worthless hound you wanted to marry me to; the years of sneaking and spying—I throw all that in your face. He has no claim on me," she went on swiftly to Brender. "By my father—I'm an American. I escaped into my country. He followed me and stole me away again. He's carrying me back to Mexico, where the courts will give him the sort of rulings that he pays for. Let me have five minutes with an American court and I'm free from him forever!"

"You'll have all the time you want—and all the freedom," said Brender. "Turn your face to the wall, Murcio. If I have to look at it any more, I'm going to change it with my gun."

That outburst made Murcio turn suddenly, and he leaned against the wall as though he needed that support.

He kept whispering and gasping, with a sob bubbling up and down in his throat. "It can't happen—it cannot be— not on the verge of success—that she should be swept away from me—wealth, ease—oh, my hopes!"

Here his voice was altered as Brender, with a few lengths of cord from his pocket, trussed Murcio foot and hand, and laid him on the floor. Murcio's own handkerchief was balled up and thrust at his mouth. He put his teeth together and fought against the gag. Brender had to tap the teeth with the barrel of his revolver before the Mexican opened his mouth to gasp. That instant the gag was inserted. And, with eyes that bulged with hysterical fear, Murcio stared at Brender. The Mexican's face began to swell and turn purple.

"Listen," said Brender. "If you lie calmly, you'll be able to breathe perfectly well. But if you lose your nerve and start fighting, you're going to choke yourself. I hope you do!"

He took the girl by the arm.

"He won't choke?" she whispered.

"No. Except with fright. Is *he* your uncle?"

"Only by courtesy. He's the guardian that bad luck gave

me. Listen to me. If we try to leave by the hall, they're sure to see us. What shall we do?"

"The window?" he suggested.

"The lamp has to burn there all night, and a man outside is watching it, to make sure that I don't try to leave in that way."

"We'll have to chance the hall to get to another room," he told her. "Come!"

She had pulled a broad-brimmed hat over her head. Through the deep shadow it made he could only guess at her face, but he knew that she was smiling.

He opened the door. The hall was empty. The flame had burned the wick of the hanging lamp low, so that the light was cast from it in long, tremulous waves. And it seemed to Brender that the metal knobs of the doors glimmered at him like watching eyes.

They crossed the hall quickly, and he turned through the doorway of the room by which he had entered the house. The moonlight was slanting more deeply through the window, and as they went toward it, he tore the spread from the bed and twirled it into a clumsy rope.

"You can slide down by this," he told her. "Are you strong in the hands?"

She closed her hand on his wrist. It was like the grip of a hard-fingered boy.

"Good," said he. "When you reach the ground, don't wait for me, but start around under the arcade; keep in the shadow. Go to the patio gate and start climbing it. Use the iron crossbars that strengthen it. Take off your shoes. We have to be as soft as shadows."

Her shoes rattled lightly against the floor as she snatched them off. She slipped over the sill of the window as he tossed out the length of the twisted bed covering. He had tied a knot in his end of it, and held it with a firm grip. And she, gripping the cloth with her hands and twisting her legs around it, cast up at him one frightened glance, then smiled.

His whole heart went out to that smile with a sudden rush.

She disappeared. Smoothly her weight descended, and then the cloth recoiled upward a little as the strain on it ceased.

He snatched it inside, and was himself instantly out the window. It was not easy work. But he had left his boots in the room, and his stockinged feet gripped the ledge of the window eaves below him more securely.

A moment later, from those very eaves he slipped. His handhold hardly delayed his fall.

But he had wit enough to loosen his body, and when he struck the pavement, it was lightly, on his feet. The impact crumbled the power out of his legs. He bunched up on hands and knees, then rose, unhurt, and saw the girl fleeing, a shadow within shadows, under the arcade.

For his own part, he disregarded the advice which he had given to her, and raced straight across the patio, taking extra chances, for it seemed to him that the entire house *must* waken at any moment. He should have bound Murcio to the foot of the bed. By this time he must have rolled across the floor and begun to kick at the door with his feet.

Brender and the girl reached the heavy, closed gate of the patio at the same time. She was panting, but her face was not strained by fear. She gave him one glance of companionship, and trust, and gratitude, and then started to climb.

Instantly a voice said, outside the patio gate: "Now what fool is shaking the gate at this time of night?"

X

In the Dark

THE girl dropped noiselessly back to the ground. Fear had struck her this time, and she spilled loosely against the side of Brender, shuddering.

"Who's there?" bawled the voice outside the gate.

In spite of fear, she managed to whisper:

"Alonso Santos!"

"Alonso Santos," said Brender. "To test the lock of the gate."

"Señor Santos?" exclaimed the guard outside. "I should

never have known your voice. Will you open the gate and speak to me, señor?"

"Stand your guard," said Brender, deepening his voice a little. "Keep your eyes open and your wits about you. I have other things to do than waste time."

He heard the other muttering some sort of protest, for it seemed that the second voice of Brender had been no more like the accents of Santos than his first speech. In the meantime, he was stealing back under the arcade with the girl.

He had to keep an arm around her. Sickening fear made her waver and stumble as she walked.

When they were deep in the shadow he took the softness of her chin between thumb and forefinger and gave it such pressure that he felt the sharp edge of the bone beneath that velvet of flesh. She gasped at the pain, and he dropped his hand. She had thrown her head back to escape from the torment, and she kept it back now, staring at him. The shuddering of her body had stopped.

"It's your happiness and my life," said Brender in a murmur. "If you fail yourself now, you fail both of us."

"Go on by yourself," she said. "I'm better now, but I can't trust myself. I may give way. I'm afraid when the test comes that I'll crumble inside, as I did just now. Go on and get yourself out of trouble. Because if they find you, they'll murder you instantly! There's no mercy in them. I mean wealth to them if they can force me south over the border. They'd blot out twenty men to take me back, and they'd kill you like a dog. Go, go!"

"You're over the panic now," he told her. "Grit your teeth. You've got to come through with me."

"I'll wilt again, as I did just now," she gasped. "When I heard the voice of him, everything went to pieces in me. Go by yourself. God bless you! I'm not worth the saving."

He looked desperately away from her. What he saw was printed forever in his mind, though the picture of the moon-whitened face of the hotel on one side and the black wall on the other, with blacker windows let into it meant nothing to him. Beyond, there was the night blue of the sky, washed by moonlight, and one yellow planet swimming in it. He saw that picture while he thought of the next chance. There was a corner door, he remembered, that opened off the patio and led through a crooked hallway back to the stable. In the stable they could get horses, saddles—and then away!

Once clear of this little green paradise in the middle of the desert, with horses galloping, with this girl beside him, the most blasting heat on the widest alkali waste would be a heaven to him.

And still she was telling him to go, urging him away with her hands.

He took her by both wrists.

"We give them the slip together, or we're caught together," he said. "You understand? Quick, now, and come with me! There's only one end for the two of us!"

The next moment she was running beside him around the shadowy arcade, their feet whispering over the tiles. And as she ran, he saw that her hands were balled into small, tight fists. But the weakness had gone out of her, and her step was full of springing lightness.

They came to the corner door, where he paused and tried the knob. It stuck. He pressed with the weight of his shoulder and heard the bolt of the lock clink lightly against metal. That way was closed to them!

Should they try to climb the wall to the window above and so work through the house to a different exit?

The thought seemed impossible.

He tested the next window. It resisted his effort to raise it. He stepped back with a faint groan. And he heard the girl say:

"Are you trapped? Is there no way out? Are you lost?"

If he smashed in the window-pane, turned the catch, perhaps they could run through the room, get into the crooked hallway, and so to the stable—and the first step toward freedom. His mind was beginning to blur. The terrible cold mist of fear began to draw into his lungs with every breath he took. Hardly knowing what he did, he tried the window again with all his might.

It yielded suddenly! It made a deep, grunting noise, like that of a startled pig. And a moment later he had worked it up and was helping the girl through into the thick blackness of the interior.

He joined her there. The warm, stale air closed about him like imprisoning hands. He had made another step toward freedom and escape, with her, but still the goal seemed to be at a great distance away.

He lighted a match. The light that spurted out of the

shielding hollow of his hands struck the wall, trailed across a bed, a table, two chairs, and then glinted on the knob of a door.

It was not locked and it opened on thick blackness. With the last of the light on the match he discovered the narrow, winding corridor which, he knew, led to the stable. And now, for the first time, he felt real hope.

"We're almost to horses—almost at the door of escape!" he told the girl. "Now, soft and steady. Not a whisper. We'll soon be there. Keep hold on my coat. Walk right behind me!"

He started through the darkness, stretching out his hands so that he was in touch with the walls on either side, and at his back was the hand of the girl, as she followed. Yet he almost struck his forehead heavily against the door that ended the corridor.

This, in turn, was unlocked, and when he pushed it open, the pungent stable odor came up to his nostrils, mixed with the sweetness of well-cured hay. Some of the horses had not finished with their well-filled mangers, and he could hear the whispering sound as the hay was gathered under their lips, and the steady, rhythmical grinding of the great jaws.

Peace, surety came flooding over Brender's soul.

A few moments more, and they would be in the open, racing side by side toward freedom!

One lantern was burning. Its wick was turned so low that it made all the interior of the big stable look like a shapeless mass of shadows, but he knew the way to his mare, and found Chinook at once, with her saddle hung up on the peg behind her.

"Go to the door—that one yonder," he whispered to the girl. "Go like a snake in grass, because it may be guarded. If you find any one, come back to me. If you don't find any one, wait there, and I'll bring on the horses. Quickly!"

She was gone, instantly fading out, then looming again, dimly, against the moonlight that filled in the square of the open door.

He saddled the mare and bridled her. Near by he saw a big, rangy animal. He could not venture on lighting a candle, but with his wise hands, in the darkness, he read the slope of the shoulders, and got the hard, clean feel of the bone in the cannon.

That horse he saddled for the girl, untied the pair, and

led them cautiously back down the aisle between the stalls. She had not returned, and therefore the way was clear.

Stepping into the doorway, he was amazed that she was not standing there!

"Rose!" he whispered. "Rose?"

Something whispered in the air just behind him. Chinook threw up her head with a grunt. And as he turned about, he saw the shadow of a man's form in the darkness, and the shadowy loom of the blow that was aimed at his head. It came home. A wave of fire burst across his brain, and he fell on his face.

XI

Christian's Scheme

WHEN Brender opened his eyes again, he was in a lamplit room where the air was very warm. And a voice was drawling:

"Put in some more coffee. I want a hot shot. I'm sleepy, the way we been riding!"

Brender closed his eyes again. The pain that shot through his head with every pulse of his blood made him squint. The voice was familiar. He had heard it somewhere, and many times.

"That coffee's going to be like lye," said another voice.

It was "Buck." It was he of the prominent teeth and the smile that was continually enforced by their projection. Brender forgot his pain, and looking wildly around him, he discovered that he was stretched on the kitchen floor. Its surface had been newly scrubbed, and was still dark with moisture in places. There were worn spots ground deep in the tiling near the stove and by the sink. Two men sat at the table. Another was at the stove, and as the latter turned, Brender recognized "Stew."

That fleshy forehead and brutal face made Brender's heart sink. Only on the most savage missions did Christian use Stew. Where a death was wanted, that gun artist was employed, but not in lesser things.

And his presence here meant, with that of Buck, that Christian's men had successfully followed the trail—in the moonlight! Or had they merely guessed at the destination of the fugitive?

He groaned involuntarily.

"Hullo!" said the voice of Buck.

And the tall, cranelike form leaned from a chair.

"He's come to," said Buck. "Here he is, chief!"

The chief?

Yes, there was Christian with that pale, lean, handsome face and the hair worn long, like an artist's. There was the half-thoughtful look of the artist about all his features, too, and the same sensitive mouth, the same slight stiffness of the upper lip. When he spoke, his nostrils were continually pinching in, or flaring a little. The whole face became fluid and expressive, from the mouth to the supple eyebrows, and the wrathful or quizzical brow. Every emotion could be registered there, or else every show of emotion could be banished from his face.

Barry Christian stood up and made a movement with his hand.

"Put him on the table," he said.

Buck and Stew lifted the trussed body of Brender and sat him on the edge of the table, so that his eyes were level with those of Christian, who passed delicately sensitive fingers over the head of his captive and drew in a deprecatory breath.

"Too hard, Buck," he said. "You have no sense of touch. Much too hard. A little farther back—here, you see—and that blow would have smashed the skull like a shell. A very hard blow! Much too hard."

"Sorry," said Buck gloomily. And his big, pale eyes looked at Brender with deathless venom.

Another voice said: "Well, well, well, and here you are, Rap! Here you are, my poor, misguided lad! Ha, ha, ha! Poor Rap! You see that I was right, Barry?"

That was Doc Shore, brushing dust from his divided beard with the tips of his fingers and peering down at the captive out of his pink-rimmed eyes.

"You're always right, Doc," said Barry Christian.

"It's worth the ride out here, to be in at the death—and to know that I was right when I guessed that he would come to Higgins's place. Oh, Barry, I know the heart of a young man. My body is old, perhaps, but my heart is still young."

He laughed again, and then waved his hand.

"So long, Rap," he said. "I'll be seeing you later."

And he walked out of sight.

"How are you, Rap?" asked Christian tenderly. "Are you in much pain?"

Hope shot up in the breast of Brender. That gentle voice might mean nothing. The hypocrisy of Christian was a bottomless pit. And yet who could read his mind beforehand? He might choose to regard this whole affair as a mere explosion of boyish enthusiasm and make light of the escapade.

"I'm a bit dizzy," said Brender. "That's all. There's not much pain."

"Good!" said Christian. "I'm glad of that. I wouldn't want you to be out of your head with pain, because I have to talk to you a little, my boy."

He added: "Here, Stew. Give Rap a swallow of coffee. Coffee is great stuff to clear the head, eh?"

"I'd rather give him a swaller of boiled lead," said Stew.

"Hush, Stew!" said Christian. "Boiling lead?"

He laid his hand over his breast, the delicately tapered fingers moving slowly.

"Boiling lead! You're a rough fellow, Stew," said the chief.

"Rough?" said Stew. "I'd like to use a rasp on him and rub him down to the bone, I would. You dirty snake!" he added to Brender, as he brought the coffee cup.

"Be quiet, Stew," said the gentle voice of Christian. And he took the cup and put it to the eager lips of Brender, saying: "A young chap like Rap is sure to boil over, now and then. Too much enthusiasm. Too much spirit. A little too mercurial. But on the other hand, think of the many good turns he's done for us all. There's hardly been a more valuable man for all of us, than Rap has been since he joined our little company."

"Are you going to talk like that about him?" asked Stew, thrusting out his bulldog face.

"And why not?" said Christian. "Why shouldn't I talk about him like this?"

There was just the slightest elevation of his head, the slightest change and hardening of his voice, but it was enough to make Stew wince back half a step and hold his tongue.

If the men of Christian knew nothing else, they knew how to read the face of their master carefully and tell when trouble was in the air. For this soft-spoken devil had struck men dead with a smile still on his lips and then wiped the blood from his hands and carried on from that point in his sentence where he had been interrupted.

"There!" said Christian soothingly. "There, Rap. Isn't that better, now that you have a little hot coffee under the belt?"

"A lot better. Thanks!" said Brender.

Lifting his eyes, he looked earnestly into the face of the chief. An unfathomably angelic smile answered him, a softening of the eyes, a tenderness about the mouth. There was something fatherly and protective in the whole semblance of the man.

If only he could trust to that expression, all was well! All that had happened was as nothing!

"I'm glad you feel better," said Christian. "Are you well enough to talk to me a little, Rap?"

"Yes," said Brender. "All you want. I wanted to tell you, too, about Silvertip and the restaurant, back there in Copper Creek."

"Ah, I understand, I understand!" said the outlaw chief. "What? A young lad—clean-cut young one. Murder! He thought that as he walked in, didn't you, Rap? And murder of whom? Why, of a famous man—of the great Silver, himself. And a fine-looking fellow Silver is, with an eye that men won't forget. A man of character, a man of sense and decency. Isn't that the look of him, Rap?"

"It is," said Rap. His enthusiasm swept up and controlled him. "He saw what was coming to him, chief. He saw what was coming, and he got ready to take it, like a man. If you'd been there, you would have called the deal off. There was no yellow in Silvertip. He just turned in his chair and looked around him. He saw there were four of us. He saw we were planted on him. But he didn't buckle under. And all at once I couldn't go ahead with the thing."

"Of course you couldn't," murmured Christian. "My dear boy, of course you couldn't. It seemed rotten and low, didn't it?"

"Yes, it did," agreed Brender.

"And since it seemed rotten and low, of course you couldn't go ahead with it. To have tackled him alone, now—that would have been better for you. You wouldn't have minded that so much, of course. It would have seemed more gentlemanly. A duel, not a massacre."

"A duel *and* a massacre," said Brender with a wry smile. "I wouldn't have a chance in front of him. Nobody would. He's fast as lightning, and he can see in the dark, pretty near."

"Nobody would have a chance with him?" murmured Christian, lifting those mobile brows of his in an expression of almost childish wonder. He chose to ignore his former contests with Silver, keeping within his own breast the hatred and admiration he felt for him. Those of his men who knew of the past dared not open their lips. Almost by sheer force of his determination, Christian had erased from men's minds the defeats of the past. "Nobody?" repeated Barry Christian.

"Except you," said Brender hastily, remembering certain things that he had seen, and many others that he had heard about.

"Ah, don't flatter me, Rap," said Christian gently. "Whatever you do, don't flatter me. Flattery is the worst mental poison in this world. The worst of all. The greatest men have gone down before the flattery of their friends, when the swords and the guns of their enemies couldn't destroy them! No, no, flattery is the worst of all! You won't flatter me, Rap, will you?"

Brender shook his head.

"Are you laughing at me, chief?" he asked. "You know that nobody in the world can stand up to you."

"Nobody? Ah, ah, the world is larger than we are," said the criminal. "I should never pretend that *nobody* can stand up against me. All I know is that I keep myself in practice, patiently, every day, working away my hours." He sighed. "A little natural talent, and constant preparation. That's all it needs. You fellows are my equals, every one of you. Taking a little pains is all the difference between us. But now, Rap, to return to your friend Silvertip. Where did he hide out when he came to the Higgins place with you?"

"He didn't come here," said Brender.

"Ah, he didn't come? He deserted you, Rap? Well, well, I should not have expected that of the great Silver. Not the sort of a fellow who would desert a friend when the friend is apt to get into trouble."

"He didn't run away from me," said Brender. "But I knew that I'd be running into a lot of trouble, before long."

"You knew it?" said the soft voice of the chief.

"I knew it. I knew that I couldn't beat you, chief. I knew that you'd presently run me down. I thought there was no use putting Silver in the bag with me. And that when you caught me, there was no use in Silver being shot to pieces fighting for my hide. So I pulled out away from him, in the middle of the night, and came on by myself. He doesn't know this part of the world very well, and he'll never find me here."

"Ah," said Christian, "You guessed that we'd be a lot keener to get at you than to get at Silver, didn't you?"

"Well, you'd call me a traitor. I knew that," said Brender. "I knew that I'd get the red mark on my name."

"He knew that," said Christian to the others, without the slightest emphasis.

"Are you going to keep talking to him? Ain't you going to let me get at him?" demanded Stew.

The leader silenced Stew with a gesture.

"We guessed that you'd come here," said Christian. "I don't know how. When I thought of your happy nature, Rap, and your jolly, carefree ways, I suddenly had a picture of you sitting in the cool of Higgins's patio and drinking his liquor and taking your ease. So we came here and saw Higgins, who kindly took us up to your room. But you were not there. However, when we found your horse in the stable, we could guess that you had not actually left the place. So we waited. And first came the pretty girl, and then came our handsome Rap Brender.

"I'm sorry that Stew hit you so hard. I would have handled the job myself, but my hands were full, just then, managing the girl, and keeping her silent. Valiant little thing, Rap. She kept struggling, and fighting, and trying to free herself, and shout a warning to you. How her heart beat! How she moaned, deep in her throat. It was touching. I pitied her. I envied you, Rap, too. Lovely little thing. Delightful hands. Delicate hands!"

He smiled at Brender after a fashion that he had, tilting his head back, and half closing his eyes, and letting his lips part a little, slowly, until the white of his teeth flashed through. Brender had seen that smile on the face of the chief when he knew that death was in his heart.

"Where is she now?" asked Rap Brender. "Was she hurt? Was she harmed?"

"Look, Stew," said the chief with a sort of tender amusement. "Rap is all of a tremble, afraid that the girl was hurt. No, no, she was as safe in my hands as a small bird in its nest. Just as safe, I give you my word. And then I just turned her over to her guardian. Ah, Rap, a bad business that, taking young girls away from their lawfully appointed guardians."

"He's not!" exclaimed Brender. "The fellow lied to you, chief. I swear that he lied! She ought to be a free citizen of our country. She's American, and they're going to take her south to Mexico, and make her do what they please, and crush the money out of her! She's rich, and they want to get her money. It's an outrage! If you stop them, she'll reward you!"

"She'll reward me? Well, well," said the chief. "Perhaps she would, after all. Though I suppose that good actions should reward themselves. But she's rich, is she? Ah, ah—rich and an orphan, and so brave, and so fierce to save Rap Brender from harm! It's a touching case, and I think that I shall have to do something about it. I'm sure that I shall. I give you my word that you may rest assured, Rap—that I'll do something about it. Just what, I don't know—but certainly Mr. Murcio shall hear from me!"

"And this here skunk?" asked Stew.

Buck turned his pale, hungry eyes on Brender at the same moment.

"What would you have me do?" asked Barry Christian.

"I'd have you back out and leave him to me for a coupla hours," said Stew. "These here walls are pretty thick. We wouldn't disturb nobody very much while we was working on him."

Buck swallowed, then he licked his dry lips and continued to run his eager eyes over and over the body of Brender.

"But would it be wise?" said Barry Christian. "You must remember that as long as we hold Rap in our hands, Silvertip is drawing closer and closer to us. He is searching for his vanished friend. He is combing the desert, on that matchless horse of his, like a hawk in the air, hunting, hunting, never at rest. Such a man as Silver, you know, will never give up, so long as sacred friendship is in his mind, so long as a sacred obligation remains to be discharged. No, he'll continue hunting until he finds Rap Brender, and when he finds Rap, then, lads, we close our hands over the most interesting man in this entire world; we close our hands over Silver himself."

He stood up suddenly. His thoughts for an instant struck through the profound mask of his hypocrisy like white fire through a storm cloud. And the keen, penetrating light shot from his eyes.

Stew and Buck looked at their chief, aghast.

"He had the world before him. He could wander where he pleased," said Christian. "But he chose to interfere with me—and therefore, he is dead! He is a ghost already. He throws no shadow on the sand!"

The passion faded suddenly out of his eyes.

"To catch this priceless Silver," said the chief, "would be more than our united talents might be able to accomplish, my friends. But now, on account of Mr. Brender, we don't need to plan and scheme and wear out our horses pursuing him. We may simply wait here until the profound mind of Silver has solved the problem and located the man. We then pull the trigger, and the trap falls, and Silver is ours, taken like an eagle out of the sky."

He dropped an affectionate hand on the shoulder of Stew.

"And after that happens, Stew," he said, "after that happens, we may perhaps be able to do something about Rap Brender himself. Because I know what you have in mind, Stew, and I have such an affection for you that it would pain me to disappoint you."

He smiled at Stew, at Buck, and, last of all, and most lingeringly and tenderly, on Rap Brender himself.

So that Rap, bowing his head suddenly, felt the ice of despair slipping like a bitter steel edge into his heart.

XII

Higgins's Barroom

THERE was only one part of his estate where Tom Higgins was perfectly at home. When he walked through the green of his flourishing fields and groves, he always felt a little incredulous of his good fortune; when he wandered through his house, he could not believe that Tom Higgins had built it, but when he worked as bartender in his own saloon, he was thoroughly content.

He had furnished the place carefully. The bar itself was a ponderous structure with a good, heavy brass rail running in front of it to uphold the boots of customers, and no matter what other work was performed on the place each day, that brass rod had to be burnished until it shone like a flame.

Across the wall behind the bar ran a great mirror, in three neatly joined sections, and in front of that mirror stood three ranks of parti-colored bottles. They had been collected for their colors, in fact, rather than for their contents. They all contained liquor of one sort or another, but even Tom Higgins had forgotten what was in most of them. What delighted him was the number and the variety of the host.

He was swabbing off the surface of his bar, on this day, not because it needed swabbing, but because out of his youth he retained mental pictures of competent bartenders swabbing off their bars with a fine, broad flourish of the arm. Besides, he liked to throw a little water on the bar and then polish it off, because he felt that the red-brown of the surface came up with a smoother polish, that reflected the window lights more deeply and clearly, as well as the dim golden lettering that ran across the mirror behind him.

Tom Higgins would have been glad to chat, but there

was in the room only the tall and military form of the big Mexican, Alonso Santos. The other Mexican, the real leader of the strange party, Murcio, had just been called out of the saloon by Barry Christian.

It was while Tom was rubbing up his bar that a flash of gold gleamed beyond his swinging doors. And a moment later, when the doors were pushed open, he saw what was in fact a golden stallion, stockinged in black to the knees and the hocks.

There was only a flash of the horse, but that glimpse made the heart of Tom Higgins jump. Then he took heed of the man who was entering. For he was worth a look. He might be twenty-five. He might be thirty. But plainly he was in the very prime of life. The face was brown, deeply sun-tanned, and aggressive in cut of features, and yet with a comfortable solidity about the bony frame that suggested that this man could endure a battering. But, above all, the watchful Tom Higgins was delighted with the fellow's build. For about the neck and arms and shoulders there was the weight of luxurious power, and then the rest of the body ran away to the lean, stringy hips of the perfect athlete. Merely to watch the man walk was a thing to light the eyes, there was such a rising on the toes, such suggestion of speed and grace and strength combined.

The stranger paused just inside the door and knocked from his clothes some of the desert dust that had accumulated in every wrinkle. He took off his sombrero and dusted that, also, exposing at the same time the massive size of his head, and two singular markings of gray above the temples, ridiculously like incipient horns about to break through the hair. That suggestion of horns was perhaps the thing that made the man seem formidable, crafty, full of devices.

Had not Tom Higgins heard of such a man, not long before? The gray spots in the hair—and a golden stallion?

"Glad to see you, brother," said Tom Higgins.

"How's things?" responded the other, coming to rest at the bar with his left elbow on it, and a shoulder slumping as one foot was fitted upon the brass rail beneath.

"Pretty fair—pretty fair," said Higgins.

"Beer, please," the stranger ordered.

"You'll find it cold, too," said Higgins. "Same cold as spring water. I got a pipe running here from deep in the spring, and that water it flows around the beer bottles day and night and never stops cooling 'em off."

"Have some with me," suggested the stranger.

Higgins pursed his lips. There was no room in his small face for more than one large feature, and this was the mouth, wide and thick as the lips of a Negro. When Higgins laughed, one could see of him no more than the gaping mouth, the teeth, and a few wrinkles around the margin of the picture.

"It ain't my time of day for beer," he asserted. "But I'll have a shot of red-eye with you. Real rye, boy, and ten years old."

He dumped a finger of the rye into the bottom of a whisky glass and raised it with one hand, while with the other he poured the frothing beer into a tall glass for his client and approved with his eye of the dew that gathered on the sides of the glass.

"And here's how," said the stranger.

"How!" said Higgins.

He tossed off his drink, and then grinned as he saw the big fellow slowly draining the contents of his glass until he put it down half empty, and sighed with pleasure.

"Who's been through here lately?" asked the stranger.

"Why, just the ordinary string of folks that cross the desert and wanta stop over," said Tom Higgins, instantly cautious. "Know many folks around this part of the world?"

"Not many," said the stranger. "There's a fellow called Rap Brender, though."

Tom Higgins started. He looked suddenly down, as though he might betray something with his face.

"Brender," he said. "Lemme see. Youngish, sort of. Dark and mighty good-looking."

"That's it."

"Well," said Tom Higgins, "he's been here, all right. Matter of fact, he was here the other day. And matter of fact, he's coming back!"

"When?"

"Why, I dunno. I think he said in a day or so. Maybe this evening."

"Well," said the stranger, "I'll take another bottle of beer into your back room and sit there in the cool for a moment, if you don't mind."

"Help yourself," answered Higgins.

He went as far as the door and made a hospitable gesture.

"Just make yourself at home," said Higgins.

He saw the other seated, and then went back to the bar.

He found that the big head of the Mexican was nodding at him.

"That's the man!" said Santos, very softly. "That must be the man that Mr. Christian wants and that we're all to look out for. That must be Silvertip!"

"It's him!" whispered Higgins.

Silvertip, in the meantime, sat in the back room of the saloon, by no means free from apprehension. He was by force of long-endured dangers about as suspicious as a hunting wolf, or a fleeting moose, and he had not failed to notice the start with which the bartender had heard the mention of the name of Rap Brender.

Silver tried to diagnose the case as he sat in the dimness of the little room. Huge, round-headed trees covered the field before his eyes. Between the trunks, he could see the sunset colors begin to tarnish the bright edge of the sky. And back and forth under the trees two men were walking, one tall, with a pale face and long black hair, and the other short, stodgy, with tightly puffed cheeks and a bristling little mustache.

Silver noted them as they wandered here and there, conversing busily. The short man was arguing with fierce heat. The tall man spoke in conciliatory tones, in a gentle voice, with graceful and soothing gestures. Yet his companion refused to be soothed.

But there was the problem of the bartender to be solved for Silver himself. The man knew Rap Brender. And why the start? Well, perhaps the bartender might think that he was an officer of the law, pursuing Brender. Or perhaps it was simply that the man was afraid of Rap.

In any case, it was strange that such a direct inquiry had received such a direct answer. People who knew an outlaw like Rap Brender were more apt to fence for a time before they admitted their acquaintance. But the bartender had spoken as though he were stuttering through a memorized piece.

That was the thing on which the suspicions of Silver centered. The peculiarity of voice and manner, the total lack of normalcy, the sudden change from a hearty bartender to the stuttering hulk of a man that had to look down to the floor, utterly embarrassed.

It was a small thing perhaps, but Silver knew that the greatest causes might be wrecked by a failure to explore just such small reefs as this seemed to be.

Slowly, carefully, he recalled every feature of the conversation. His mind reverted to the big, dignified Mexican who had been sitting at the side table. There was probably a story worth the telling behind that fellow, too, with his military bearing, and his costly clothes, and his air of command. He was no random prospector or cowpuncher or cattle dealer who had made the short cut across the desert and stopped off at this oasis.

In fact, an air of guilty mystery began to gather about the place, in Silver's mind, and he slid his hand quickly up under his coat, to enjoy the reassuring touch of his fingers against the rough butt of the weapon.

His thoughts were taken from his own position and Brender by the approach of the tall man and the fellow with the brown, puffed cheeks. When they got nearer, Silver knew what he had suspected before—the tall one was Barry Christian!

The little fellow was saying: "This is the end of the argument—señor, it is the end! The point of it is—what I have done, I have done without you. That is true, no? Until last night you gave me a little help!"

"Ah, Murcio," said the other, in his wonderfully gentle, rather sad voice. "Ah, Murcio, will you tell me that it was nothing? Only a *little* help when you were about to lose your prize, when it was about to slip away?"

"They could not have gone far," argued Murcio. "They could have been tracked. Not even the desert could have swallowed them. I should have found them again!"

"Stubborn fellow—stubborn Murcio," said the tall man gently. And he laid his hand lightly on the shoulder of the Mexican.

"A woman could not have ridden very far—not through the heat of the desert. She would have failed. We would have recaptured her!"

"Ah, but she's a strong little thing," said the other. "Full of strings and fibers of strength. She would endure like a mustang. Never trust to her weakness, or you'll be sadly surprised. No, never trust to that! But what I ask from you, Murcio, I ask against my will. It is simply that I am a business man."

"A business man? Do you call it business? Blackmail!" exclaimed Murcio.

"A business man," said the soft, steady voice of the American. "A business man, like yourself, eh?"

Murcio stuck his hands together above his head and groaned.

"But for a reward—yes, yes. I shall pay you the reward—a good, fat sum. But you are asking for a fortune!"

"She has a great fortune. I'm asking only for a bit of it," said the American. "You must understand that. She is very rich. You won't need all of that money for yourself."

"I never meant to take it all!" groaned Murcio. "There must be something left for her!"

"For her?" said the tall man. "Ah, Murcio, what is her need of money? With her sweet face and her charming smile, she cannot help but find an easy way through the world. All the more delightful if she knows that men are not hunting her down for her money."

"Still you have words—still you argue!" said Murcio, staring suddenly up at his companion. "What a terrible man you are, Señor—"

Before the name was spoken, the forefinger of the tall man was lifted in a warning gesture, and Murcio snapped his teeth on the unspoken word, while the American glanced suddenly around him, and over his shoulder, straight at the open window behind which Silver was sitting.

The tall man moved away with Murcio, their voices again heard, but not distinctly, while around the corner of the building came the colossal bulk of Tom Higgins, the skirts of his great white apron fluttering as he strode along.

He made gestures as he approached.

Presently he had withdrawn a bit to the side with Christian, and they spoke earnestly together.

What Higgins said, Silver could in no way make out, but the words were sufficient to make the pale-faced man turn suddenly toward the building. And again it seemed to Silver that a gun had been leveled at him.

He stood up and went through the barroom.

"Not leaving us, señor?" asked the big Mexican with a sudden strange access of courtesy.

"Only taking a ride around the place before it's dark," said Silver. "I'll be back, thank you."

Parade swept his master rapidly through the green of the oasis. Glancing back, Silver saw Alonso Santos stroll out from the saloon and stare after him, shading his eyes against the red flare of the western sky.

There were other horses tied in front of the saloon, but none of them was mounted. For that matter, who would dream of pursuing the rider of Parade except with many reliefs of horses along the way?

No, if there were danger in the oasis, he was winging safely away from it now. The long and heavy rhythm of the beating hoofs of the stallion made a Mexican woman turn to stare as he passed the little village of the laborers. She was hanging out clothes on a wash line, and she left a picture in the mind of Silver as he swept by. There were half a dozen of the little white-washed huts where the Mexicans lived. They were the men who had charge of the irrigation, because their race had been familiar with the handling of water for many hundreds of years before the Spaniards rode into Old Mexico. And now Tom Higgins kept enough of them to care for all the soil of his land.

The flashing, wet washing and the gleaming white houses swept behind Silver. He passed the last of the trees. And presently the great stride of the stallion was carrying Silver out into the desert.

He went straight on until the oasis drew into a dark patch behind him. Then he slowed Parade to a walk. There was no need for hurry. The twilight would soon cover him from any prying eyes, and at the slower pace he could put his thoughts in order more easily.

He listed his newly gained knowledge.

First, Christian! Again they were pitted against each other!

Second, in spite of all possible acting and dissimulation, he was sure that Tom Higgins knew something about Rap Brender.

Third, out of the fragments of the conversation which he had overheard, it seemed really clear that Murcio had in his possession a woman, a girl, out of whom he expected to make a great deal of money, and that Christian had helped Murcio by preventing the escape of the girl. For that help he was demanding a reward of such a size that Murcio was tortured at the mere thought of the sum. He would pay an ample reward, but he did not want to give a fifty-per-cent share in the prize. And yet, when he argued, he seemed to take it for granted that Barry Christian would be able to take what he chose before the end.

It was not Brender alone who needed help. There was this girl, also, whoever she might be.

"I would be a fool to return," said Silver to himself. "They know me now. They'll be watching for my face. I must not go back. I must try to get men together and come onto the Higgins place by force of many hands."

He shook his head as he had that thought, for he knew that long before he could cross the desert and get sufficient aid, the whole problem would be solved in another way, or else the girl would have been taken from the Higgins place. Besides, it would take a small army to force its way into Higgins's place.

What should he do, then?

Suddenly he knew, calmly, surely, but with a wave of ice-cold apprehension, exactly what he would do. He would turn straight back toward the oasis toward the tremendous danger that was Christian, and under the cover of night, use his wits to unlock a sufficiency of doors until he had found the girl that was in Murcio's charge.

But he could not return with an unaltered appearance.

He made his changes quickly. He dismounted, stripped, and rubbed himself thoroughly with the brown of a liquid that he took from a small bottle. He took from a saddle-bag a black wig—it was not the first time that he had turned himself into a Mexican—and fitted it onto his head. It left him with a lowered forehead and a shag of black hair falling down to the nape of his neck and over his eyes. He blackened his brows, and deftly and carefully blackened his eyelashes, also. And now, if he kept from staring at people, it would be very hard, by artificial light, to note that his eyes were of a pale color.

He took out a little round mirror, and, since the sun had now gone so far down that only a few murky, ochre-colored lights gleamed in the sky, he lighted a match and examined his make-up in this manner. There were several alterations that had to be made. Here and there the stain had gone on his skin in streaks, leaving darker and lighter spots. The variations might not be noticed at night, but he had to make himself as perfect as possible. For suppose Christian were to give him one glance?

He was making his plan little by little—mere strokes of light here and there against a great darkness—as he put on his outer clothes, stuffed the rest into his roll behind the saddle, and turned the head of Parade back toward the oasis.

As he came closer again, as the trees grew great before him, each blotting out a rounded section of the stars, it seemed to Silver that the whisper of the wind was the murmur of human voices, and that dark forms were crouching there in the shadows, ready to start out at him.

He made himself ride boldly through these shadows, but still shudders were working up and down the flesh of his back as he put the trees behind him. He wanted to look around, half expecting to see armed men gliding out on his trail, shutting him into a trap. He set his teeth against that weakness so hard that a fine perspiration broke out on him.

If this was how he felt in the beginning, how would it be when he came close to the lights of the house that were glimmering in the distance?

He told himself that he was only half a man, but he could hardly shame himself into a greater confidence.

In the next grove he left Parade. He stripped the bridle from the head of the stallion and stuffed it into a saddle-bag. Then for a moment he remained stroking the head of the horse, filled with gloomy thought.

It was too much to ask of any man, he declared to himself. Before him there was no really tangible prospect of success. He would be like a blindfolded man fumbling in a room where enemies are at watch with a light to help them.

Yet in spite of himself, he found that he had left Parade and was walking forward from the grove and toward the starry lamps that shone from the house of Tom Higgins!

XIII

The Lure of the Lamp

HE made a detour toward the little cluster of Mexican huts. This meant careful work, for the children were out playing in the dark, their half-naked bodies flashing again and again across the shafts of golden lamp-light, and they had a troop of mongrel dogs with them, leaping and scurrying here and there.

He moved like a snake around the house and came to the wash line which he had noted. It made an important link in the chain that he had planned for action, for he thought that he had seen some white shirts and cotton trousers in the lot.

He was right. He stripped, trusting the dark stain on his body to keep it from being visible by the starlight, and, in fact, no human eye would have been able to locate him.

He dressed rapidly in the clothes that he had found. The shirt was small. The trousers came hardly half the distance between his knees and ankles, so he rolled them up above the knees. Shoes he would have to do without, but for that matter the Mexicans he had seen at work were either barefooted or simply in huarachos.

The shirt and trousers would have to serve him. They were still very damp, but that would have to be a point of minor importance.

His discarded clothes he rolled into a compact bundle and put them into the center of a little shrub not far from the hotel of Tom Higgins. Then he began to close on the place in circles, as a beast of prey closes in on its quarry. It was partly that he wanted to find out the best means of getting up to the house unseen, and it was partly that he wanted to examine all the lay of the land around the place in case he had to flee for his life at any moment, and from any part of the hotel.

In this manner he came around and around the hotel, and finally saw that the obvious place of approach was from the rear, through a big open court that, in turn, opened upon a patio on one side, and exposed one of the outer walls of the building on the other.

The trouble with this avenue was that it was already occupied.

The night was windless, except for small gusts that stirred up wisps of dust, and the heat of the desert, therefore, was not rolled in upon the oasis. The grass and the trees began to give out their coolness.

The windmills were silent. The big wheels were no longer purring, and the gears had stopped their rattling and clanking. Instead—since water had to be flowing night and day on the plantation—a team of three mustangs labored constantly around and around an open-mouthed well, lifting an endless chain of buckets that dumped into a trough. Steadily the drawbeam moaned against the central shaft, and the water, with continual white pulses, gushed away down the trough. The driver sat on the drawbeam itself, feeding a black snake into his three horses from time to time, for the gait was not a walk, but a shuffling trot.

The next relay of horses for the work was held by another driver near by.

Silver saw these things as he moved from bush to bush, stalking forward. Now a third man came out of the darkness and spoke to the driver, who waited with his relief team. Silver could hear them clearly.

"Tonio," said the newcomer, "they are playing dice in Alfredo's house. I myself have won five dollars. Luck is in the air. And this is the time for you to have your revenge."

"You see where I am!" said Tonio. "I must be here with my horses!"

"Your boy can drive the team."

"A scorpion stung his foot this afternoon. He is lying groaning. You ought to know that! And how can he drive my team? But will you take them for an hour only?"

"I know what your hour would be if you started winning," said the other. "No, no! Drive your own horses. I was only telling you that the game has started."

"I thank you for nothing, then," said Tonio angrily.

Silver appeared, drifting slowly toward them through the night.

"Well," said Silver, "I would drive the team for twenty-five cents. I haven't even money for tobacco."

They both turned on him. They stared a moment. The light was dim, but by the bigness of his outline they knew him to be a formidable fellow. Perhaps there was something in the drawling nature of his Spanish that made them suspicious.

"Men who work are men with money in the pocket," said Tonio. "And who are you?"

"I am José Calderon. This very day I have walked forty miles—and not on green grass all the way. Is it work, my friends, to walk forty miles just in the hope of finding a job?"

"There is no work for you here," said Tonio stiffly. "The master wants no strangers."

"Curse him!" said Silver with apparent emotion. "I talked to him; I begged him; I crouched before him, but he would give me no hope of work."

"Where did you see him?" asked the suspicious Tonio.

"In the saloon."

"Well?"

"He cursed me like a brute because there was dust on my bare feet; he would have no dust marks on his floor, he said. I took the bandanna from my neck and got down on my hands and knees and wiped up the marks that I had made. I stood in the doorway and begged him to give me work. I said that I would work day and night for my food and no money—for my food and tobacco, until I could prove to him that I am a good man. But he would not take me!"

"Well, if he took everybody," said Tonio coldly, "the place would soon be crowded."

"Will you give me one pinch of tobacco?" he begged. "I have a paper to roll the cigarette!"

"You're a beggar," answered Tonio. "I tell by the whine in your voice. You spoke of twenty-five cents. You don't need more than five cents to buy tobacco for cigarettes. And that I'll give you if you drive these horses around and around the well until I please to come back."

"Ah, señor!" said Silver. "You are very hard, but I am very poor."

"Honest men," said Tonio, "are never as poor as all this. I make you my offer. Will you take it?"

"You are a hard man," said Silver. "But I crave for to-bacco from the pit of my stomach."

"I know how that can be, too," said Tonio more kindly. "Perhaps after all I shall give more than five cents to you. That depends on how well you handle the horses, and whether or not you have them all in the same degree of sweating when I come back. Here—now let me see you hitch them to the drawbeam!"

The driver of the team that had been working till this moment now stopped, stepped down from his place, and commenced unhooking the singletree chains from the traces. So Silver took the three mustangs of the team of Tonio around to the proper place. He held them with a grip close to the bits. They laid their ears down and tossed their heads as he compelled them to back into place.

"Well," said Tonio, "you know something, and you have strong hands."

Silver hooked up the chains rapidly to the traces.

He sat on the drawbeam, picked up the black snake, and called to the horses. They lurched into their collars. The drawbeam began to groan once more against the shaft; the endless chain of buckets began to disgorge the white pulses of water into the big trough, along which it ran swiftly and was received into a large-throated pipe, where it went swishing away, unseen.

Tonio came in behind the drawbeam and began to talk.

"Watch the gray mare," he said. "She keeps her traces taut, but she is not pulling unless her head is down."

"Ah-ha! A cheat!" said Silver, and flicked the mare with the black snake.

She shook her head and began to pull hard. Tonio laughed.

"You understand," he said. "You will do a good job if you keep your eyes open. Remember, if they are not all sweating in the same way, you get *nothing* from me! But if the gray mare sweats a little more than the rest, I shall be just as pleased. Now, there's another thing. You see the window there, with the lamp shining in it?"

"I see," said Silver.

"That lamp must continue to shine."

"If God wills that it shall," said Silver.

"The moment that it stops shining, the moment that it is put out of place, you must sound an alarm. You hear?"

"What shall I do?"

"Yell at the top of your voice. Yell for Señor Santos!"

"Yes. And then?"

"Then he will come, fool. And then you tell him that some one has disturbed the lamp. That is all. Look up at the lamp once in every round, or twice."

Silver stared up at the bright light. A great climbing vine with a trunk twisted like a rope, and thick as the stem of a tree, wound up the side of the house and cast its branches to either side of the window, where the lamp burned.

"Is there some one in that room who prays by that light?" asked Silver.

"There is a poor girl who wishes it were out, perhaps," said Tonio. "How does it come that you wear wrinkled clothes?"

"If you walked forty miles through the desert, your sweat would wrinkle your clothes," said Silver.

"There is no sweat caking that cloth," said Tonio sharply.

"No, because when I reached this place I poured water over myself," said Silver. "I was so hot that the water hissed against my hide."

Tonio laughed again softly.

"Well," he said, "now you are working honestly, and you are going to earn money—perhaps. Be diligent. Watch the window, and I shall be back here after a time."

Now that he was alone at last, Silver sighed with relief to have the sharp eyes of Tonio removed from him. As the horses made round after round of the well, the drawbeam still droning its steady song, he kept his eyes fixed on the light that flooded from the casement in the second-story window above him.

Since there was a girl kept there, one who wished that the lamp might be darkened, would she not be the one about whom Murcio had talked that evening? Was it not she that had the fortune of which Christian so much wanted a share?

But he had come here to find traces of Rap Brender, who had saved his life. All other things must wait upon that necessity.

Yet for all he knew, Brender might be many a mile from this place, riding contentedly farther and farther from the danger that he feared from Barry Christian.

If only Silver could penetrate to the meaning of Higgins's start and downward look and confused words—if only he could have heard the respectful words which had been addressed by Higgins to the pale-faced man who was Barry Christian himself.

In the meantime, the lamp shone from the casement above with a steady, insistent light. And it began to draw on Silver as with a hand.

He felt the pull of the temptation like an imp of the perverse looking upon him.

The sense of duty which had brought him to this place forbade him interfering now in the affairs of that unknown girl, and still the ferment worked in Silver, until, with a stifled groan, he knew that he must yield to the temptation.

He gave the three mustangs a slashing blow with the black snake in the hope that this encouragement would keep them at their work for a considerable time, and then ran in his bare feet toward the huge trunk of the climbing vine. The bareness of his feet would help him now. And the lightness of his clothes was an advantage, also. The only excess weight was that of the revolver which he carried strapped under the pit of his left arm, inside the open shirt. But that weight was not enough to keep him from mounting the twisted trunk of the vine like a wild cat.

As he came to the casement above he paused. The shaken branches gave off a rustling sound as though a wind were blowing through them. Below him he still heard the droning of the drawbeam as the horses pulled it on their rounds. And there was no human being in view.

He sat in the casement and peered inside past the lamp. It was a big room, quite emptily furnished. He saw the sheen of a goatskin rug on the floor, and then the body of a woman stretched face down on the bed, with her arms thrown out crookedly. So she might lie in death. Some of her hair had escaped and streamed in disorder to the side, glistening black. So she would lie, in fact, if she had been slain after a struggle and thrown down by brutal hands, to lie as she fell.

The window rose silently and easily at the touch of Silver. After what he had seen, he could not have been stayed from entering that room even if there had been armed men in it.

He lifted the lamp, put it to one side, and slithered

through. Then he drew down the window, replaced the lamp, and turned, breathing more easily.

His absence from the horses might be marked before long, but the droning noise of the water wheel gave proof that the team was still at labor. Yet even when his absence was marked, who could guess, unless his ascent had been seen, that he was here in this room where the light shone from the window.

"Señorita!" he whispered.

She was not asleep. Even that lightly spoken word made her spring up from the bed and face him. And at the sight of her face, he was glad that he had come. He laid a finger on his lips and gestured behind him toward the lamp, as though it were significant of the danger in which he stood.

She had not spoken, but stepping back toward the wall a little, she caught up her loosened hair with an instinctive gesture and wound it into place. Understanding suddenly came into her dark eyes.

"You've come through the window? Then you've been seen, and unless they sent you, you're trapped here!"

"I was not seen," said Silver, trying her with English. "The horses still pull at the water wheel. You can hear 'em. But there's no one on the driver's seat."

"Who are you? And *why* have you come?" she asked, in English.

"Because I knew that some one was here with her back against the wall. No one sent me. It was chiefly guesswork. But if you want to leave, there's an open chance by climbing down that vine that runs up the face of the house. Can you manage that?"

"You're not a Mexican," she said. "It's stain that's on your skin, not the real color."

"You have eyes," said Silver. "But will you come?"

"If you're American," she said, "don't think of me, but do something for one of your own people. He's held here. They're guarding him in the loft of the barn. Forget me. It's not my life that they want, but they'll surely murder him in the end!"

"Do you know his name?" asked Silver.

"Brender. But his name doesn't matter. He's young. He's thrown himself away trying to help me. If he dies——"

"Rap Brender?" exclaimed Silver. "And these devils are

holding him? Rap Brender? I'll find him! Is there a way through the house to the stable?"

"There is. But the house is filled with men. You couldn't pass through. Go back the way you came—"

"Hush!" said Silver, holding up a hand.

For a change had come, and a vibrant sound had left the air. He knew what it meant. The horses were no longer dragging at the water wheel, and in a moment their idleness would be known; men would surely come to inquire into the silence, and the way of retreat down the climbing vine would be under observation.

He sprang into the casement to make sure, and as he had suspected, two men were coming out of the inner patio, pointing out the stationary team to one another.

Poor Tonio would have to sweat for this. He would have a chance to wish that he had promised not pennies, but dollars, for the honest tending of his team. But now the first way of retreat was thoroughly blocked.

Silver turned back to the girl.

"They're on guard again at the water wheel," he said. "We can't go back by that way. There *must* be some chance of getting through the house."

"There's none." She shook her head. "Unless you can get across the hall and into a room that opens onto the patio—and even the inner patio is guarded now. There's no way for you! Heaven help you! Who are you, and why have you come?"

He leaned his big shoulders against the wall and turned his eyes slowly about the room.

These seconds were counting against him, he knew, but it would be worse to make a blind move than none at all. All the interior of the house was a sealed book to him. He would be stepping into darkness.

"My name is Silver," he told her. "If I drop my life here—well, it's a thing that Rap Brender saved for me not long ago. They'll have to pay something before they conclude the bargain, however."

He touched the gun under his arm, but did not draw it.

"Is the door locked?" he asked.

"From the outside. Think of something to do! You can't stay here. And there's no way for you to retreat. You're lost! One more life to them. Señor Silver—"

"Say it in English," said Silver. "Just now the Spanish hurts my ears."

A footfall came down the hall rapidly and paused at the door. The girl dared not speak. Wildly she gestured toward the big clothespress that stood at the side of the room, while she threw herself as before, face downward on the bed.

One door of the clothespress was open. Silver was instantly inside it, and hidden behind the long, shimmering folds of a yellow slicker. Over the shoulder of that coat he could see the door opened by that same Alonso Santos, that same big fellow of the mustaches and the militant carriage that Silver had seen in the saloon this day.

The Mexican tossed the door shut behind him, and the careless gesture sent a cannon-shot report through the room. The girl started up from the bed and stared wildly all about her, fixing her glance on Santos at last.

"What has happened?" she asked.

Santos shaped his mustache for a moment with one hand before he answered.

"Something odd has happened in the outer patio. It seems that a rascal of a peon called Tonio left his team at the water wheel. He was fetched out of a shed close by and swore that he left the team in the hands of another fellow all in rags, who swore that he had crossed the desert to-day in search of work from Señor Higgins. Tonio let the man drive the team while he went off to play at dice, and presently the water wheel stopped turning—the stranger was gone. And it seemed to Tom Higgins that perhaps the man might have gotten into the house. How? Well, by climbing up the big vine and disappearing through your window. Come, my dear. Have you seen the man here?"

"Is it likely?" she asked.

"I'm not talking of likelihood," said Santos. "Answer me yes or no. Have you seen him?"

Silver waited for her to lie.

Instead she fixed her glance steadily, calmly, on Santos.

"I've seen several sorts of men in this room," she said.
"What manner of man was this?"

"A big, ragged peon," said Santos.

She shook her head. "I haven't seen a Mexican in this room since supper was carried in for me."

"Which you sent out without tasting, eh?" said Santos.
"Do you worry so much about the gringo, my dear?"

Her eyes closed, or almost closed.

"What have they done with him?" she asked.

"Nothing, Rosa," said Santos. "And they *will* do nothing. That is, until they've used him as a bait. It appears that he has a friend, a certain famous vagabond called Silver. And there is such a devotion between the two gringos, that since this Brender is caught and held, the other one, the important one, is sure to put his head into the trap. So they'll hold Brender until Silver appears, and then they may have the pleasure of dying together. That, I think, is the design of Mr. Christian."

"And who is Mr. Christian?" asked the girl calmly, as though the rest of the speech had meant nothing to her.

"He is a tall fellow with a pale face, and a soft voice, and the soul of a tiger, and the brain of a bloodless fiend," said Santos. "But now I must look at the casement and open the window to make sure that there are no traces on the sill."

He crossed the room out of Silver's sight, and presently there was a slight sound as the sash of the window was raised. Silver stepped instantly from his concealment.

He carried a revolver in his hand, and it was well for Santos that at that moment he was sprawling far out onto the deep casement, pushing the lamp to one side as he looked down at the upper branches and the foliage of the climbing vine.

So Silver went sidling to the door, his step soundless, his eyes flashing from the girl to the form in the window.

And she, her chin still in her hand, did not stir. She hardly seemed to glance at Silver, and the only sign she gave of emotion was the sudden tightening of the grip of the hand that clasped her chin.

The door yielded soundlessly to Silver's touch. He slid the revolver back beneath his armpit and stepped out into the hall, drawing the door shut behind him. As he closed it without a word, he heard Santos saying:

"On my word, I think that two of the twigs *have* been broken. The wind may have done it, perhaps. But if you—"

The closing of the door shut out the rest of that speech, and Silver found himself standing in a long corridor, lighted faintly from one end by a hanging lamp.

He came to the head of a flight of steps and ran lightly down the windings to the floor below.

Here again a hanging lamp gave light to the corridor

and showed him a door ajar. Through it he peered. It was a bedroom, and vacant, so far as he could see. But all was dim before his eyes, since what light entered the chamber came from lanterns in the outer patio, which was just beyond this wall.

He entered, closing the door, and remained for a moment drawing his breath. Then he passed to the window.

Beyond it he saw that the team at the well had again commenced its rounds, and the dull snoring sound, and the pulsing gush of the water from the chain of buckets, was passing softly into the night, almost overcome by the rattling of active voices.

Another man, not poor Tonio, sat on the drawbeam, for Tonio himself was held by either hand by a stout peon, and the shirt had been pulled from his brown back. A crowd stood around him, some holding lanterns that might have helped Silver to see the scene, but there were too many shifting figures that continually stepped between him and the picture that he wanted to make out.

If he could not see Tonio clearly, he could make out the man who was master of ceremonies. He was an old Mexican with a head of pure white, and he stood now with a black snake in his hand, tucking up the sleeve over his right arm.

As he prepared to flog Tonio, he made a little speech.

"Now, my children," he said, "you will see a lesson. The señor is too kind. He is too gentle. Only now and then his great heart is moved with anger, and this is one of the few times. A wretched rascal like this Tonio must make us all have trouble. What? Would it be very much for the señor to grow disgusted with us all and march us off from our homes on this green island, this happy place? A few more lazy gamblers, dice lovers, like Tonio, and we are all ruined. For our own sakes, I am going to lay on the lash. And for the good of your lazy soul, Tonio. Stand still. Don't struggle. There are ten strokes to fall, unless you howl. And that will cost you ten more. The señor will not wish to hear you yelling like a dog under the whip!"

And the lash swung in the air like a thin shadow and fell with a spat as of two open palms striking together.

There was no cry from Tonio. And Silver, realizing that hardly any power in the world could draw the attention of the crowd from the beating, determined to use this opportunity for leaving the house. If he could get out of the outer patio and around to the stable, he could try his best to reach Brender. As for the girl—they would then have two pairs of hands to help her!

He slid through the window and dropped to the ground as the fourth blow fell. And then a sudden howl, beginning loudly, wailing away to a drone, burst from the lips of the tortured Tonio.

XIV

The Barn Loft

THE loft of the barn of Tom Higgins was built on a huge scale to match the barn itself. In that barn were sheltered, at night, scores of milch cows; and, though a great percentage of their feed was green alfalfa, there was also a huge stock of baled hay on hand for their use and for the beef cattle and the horses and the mules of Tom Higgins. For his wealth, as has been said, was almost entirely on the hoof. After the last autumn cutting of the alfalfa, that immense loft was crammed to the roof with baled hay, but earlier in the year the stock diminished a great deal, for, of course, it was a maxim with Higgins to feed out his total supply of hay each year. Time would spoil the surplus, and it was not profitable to haul the hay across the burning width of the desert to the nearest town.

That was the reason why the whole end of the loft was now free space, with a wall of bales stepping back in several sections toward the center of the barn. And in that free space Rap Brender was imprisoned. It was considered an ideal place because it removed the prisoner and his doings from the observation of house servants, and although the peons of the Higgins place were proverbial for their silence still it was preferable to have as little talk as possible about Brender.

Moreover, there was plenty of room for both the prisoner and the two guards who were kept on duty day and night, each pair taking an eight-hour shift. Three rolls of blankets had been rolled down on a quantity of hay, and the ropes that bound Brender also tied him to the big wooden pillar that rose to the support of the roof. On each side of the room there was a small dormer window, and through a trapdoor protruded the head of a ladder that led to the ground floor of the barn. Up through that open trap came the noises of the feeding animals beneath, the shouting and the cursing of the Mexican peons who tended them. But at this hour of the early night all was quiet, except for the soft rustlings of hay, and the subdued, deep sound of the grinding jaws.

It was the watch of Buck and Stew. They sat at a small table that had been brought up for their comfort, and they played blackjack, each turning a restless head now and then to keep an eye on the prisoner.

But Brender lay flat on his back, his tied hands crossed on his breast, his legs straight out as he stared at the black, monstrous shadows that crossed the rafters.

Suddenly he sat up.

Buck leaped instantly to his feet and drew a gun.

"Hey, what's the matter?" exclaimed Stew, half rising, also.

He turned his head sharply toward the window at his right. A long-drawn human howl came ringing through the night air. He hastened to the window, with Buck behind him.

"I can hear the whack of the whip," said Buck. "They're beating up a peon, I guess."

Then a voice spoke out of the dimness toward the trapdoor. They saw the head and shoulders of a man.

"A lot of blind bats!" said the voice of Barry Christian. "I could have picked off the pair of you, and no trouble at all!"

He stepped up onto the floor of the loft and came scowling toward them. But the anger which had made him break out he now controlled immediately.

He unrolled a bundle and spread on the table a coat and riding trousers, a flannel shirt, a bandanna handkerchief, and a pair of riding boots, together with a big sombrero.

"A dog was nosing around in the brush of this plantation a little while ago," he said, "and the pup began yapping, and some children who were playing unearthed this bundle out of a shrub. Take a look at it. Any of you ever see it before?"

"No," said Buck.

"Not that I know of," agreed Stew.

Christian picked up the lantern from the table and shone the light of it suddenly and closely into the face of Brender. The eyes were wide and staring, though they instantly squinted.

"*You* saw it, though!" said Christian.

"Saw it? No—I never did," said Brender, swallowing hard in the midst of his sentence.

"You—never did, eh?" mocked Christian.

He sat down at the table and gave Brender his gentle, deadly smile.

"You never saw these clothes, eh? Never? Not on a tall fellow with big shoulders! Not on a tall fellow with a fine big head on his shoulders? Not a lad by the general name of Silver?"

"Those? No!" exploded Brender violently. "Not the least bit. Nothing like his clothes! The—the—the coat's all different—the—everything's different!"

Christian smiled at him, and began to roll up the bundle again.

"That's enough," he declared. "If Silver had to lie for *you*, Rap, he'd do a better job of it than you've done."

"I tell you—I swear—" said Rap Brender.

"Ah, Rap," protested the soothing voice of Christian in his most ministerial, bedside manner. "Not perjury, dear lad. Any other sin, but not perjury. Not that! These bodies of ours may walk in a great many dark paths, but consider your immortal soul, Rap, and don't swear it away. These are the clothes of Silver. I could see the truth shine out of that handsome young face of yours."

"If those are Silver's clothes, then Silver himself ain't far away!" breathed Buck. "I knew it. I knew it minutes back. I got a puckering of the skin and a chill up the back. I knew that he was in the air!"

"Gimme a man to stand watch here, will you?" said Stew. "Look at the yaller hound, turning green under my eyes! He's scared to death. Gimme a fighting man with me, if Silver's going to be on deck pretty soon!"

Christian shook his head.

"Perhaps a little fear will keep the eyes wider, Stew," he said. "And the sort of fear that Buck feels may make his body shake—but not his gun hand. I've seen Buck tremble before this, but I never saw him miss when he was shaking! No, I'll trust to Buck. And to a few more that I'm going to send up here. Because you're right, Buck. If we have Silver's clothes, the man himself is not far off. Besides, I've been hearing a queer story about a big peon—a new man that no one knows anything about, a fellow who walked all across the desert to find a job here. A barefooted peon. And no one had brains enough to ask him how he could cross the desert in his bare feet!"

"Silver?" exclaimed Buck.

"I don't know. I'm not sure," said Christian. "But I'd give a good deal to put my eye on that same peon with the big shoulders and the narrow hips. And the *very* dark Mexican skin, too! A bit of stain will make the whitest man in the world as brown as a berry. I've been a Mexican myself more than once."

And he laughed very gently, as though he were afraid that a loud sound might disturb his listeners.

"I'll take these clothes to Higgins," he said, "and let him know what I have in mind. We'll turn out every man on the place and search for that missing peon with the broad shoulders and bare feet and the very dark skin. And if we find him—"

He snapped his fingers in the air.

"Perhaps he'll turn out to be a Silver worth more than gold to me!" continued Christian. "I'll have more men up here in a few minutes. In the meantime, use your eyes. Be awake. If Silver has actually doffed his clothes and taken a disguise, he means to try his luck and take his life in his hands. And the hands of a fellow like Silver will hold a good deal, boys. And I should—" He broke off sharply before he furnished the word which would have made admission of the events which had seared into his soul his hatred of Jim Silver.

"Keep our eyes open?" said Buck. "I'll be watching for snakes to drop off the rafters!"

"That's it," said the chief. "Be on your toes. You can't be very far wrong when you're on your toes."

He went to the head of the ladder, turned to give them all one slow, penetrating glance, and then passed down the ladder out of sight.

"Silver!" said Buck in a whisper. "Look out that window, Stew. I'll look out this one. Look as far on the roof as you can, and down the side."

They went to their appointed windows, but all that they found was the naked roof line, running off to the brightness of the stars.

They turned back and faced one another.

"Keep moving," suggested Stew. "That's the way to have your eyes open."

"Move, but move slow!" answered Buck. "Silver—I'd rather have the real devil after me! Silver!" A perceptible shudder ran through his long, frail body.

"And he'll come," said Brender with a sudden depth in his voice, as though he were ten years older in conviction, at least. "He'll come, and make short work of both of you!"

"The pair of us?" said Stew. "You talk like a young fool, and there ain't no fool worse than a young fool. There ain't no one man on earth, excepting maybe Christian, that could handle the pair of us when we got our eyes open and are looking for trouble."

They paced slowly about the floor, keeping their eyes specially fixed upon the windows and upon the open trapdoor. For it seemed that there was no other possible entrance for a grown man into that part of the loft.

"Suppose that he's hid in the hay!" said Buck.

"How'd he be able to hide there, dummy?" snapped Stew. "Tell me that—how'd he be able to hide there? You know the answer? Wasn't there people here all the day long? How'd he burrow through solid piles of baled hay, anyways?"

"Well, maybe not," said Buck, reluctantly giving up the dangerous possibility. "But he can do things that you and me wouldn't think of."

"What's that? Who's on the ladder?" asked Stew.

For the head of the ladder, projecting above the trapdoor, was visibly trembling.

Buck stood close to the trap.

"Who's there?" called Buck.

"All right—boys," said a soft voice, broken a little with panting. "I'm coming up—myself."

"All right. It's the chief," said Buck, stepping back with a sigh. "We're going to have him up here with us."

He had turned from the trapdoor with Stew, but as they looked at Brender, they saw something in his face that froze them in place. And then, behind them, the panting voice, but now harsh and clear, said:

"Shove up your hands. Shove them up slow and sure!"

They looked over their shoulders, these two guards, not to see the form of their enemy rising cautiously out of the hollow black square of the trapdoor, a revolver leveled hip-high in his hand, but to glare at one another, as though each wanted to see in the face of his companion news of that terrible fate which would come to them from the hands of Barry Christian when their chief knew that they had failed in their work.

Then, with another common impulse, they began to raise their hands.

Silver stepped closer to them, little by little.

He spoke as he watched them.

"Chinook is in the third stall to the left of the ladder," he said to Brender. "I've untied her lead rope and knotted it around her neck. I got her bridle on her, too, and she's standing fast. When you get down, take her. I found a Colt in the saddle room, and now it's in your saddle holster. Flatten yourself on the mare's back and go through the stable door at a gallop. There are men on watch beyond the door, not right at it. Go through it like a devil. I'll get a gun from one of these old chums of yours before we're through. Buck—watch your hands!"

But Buck, as his hands came to the height of his shoulders, moved them more and more slowly. A fluttering appeared in his fingers. And Silver recognized the workings of a desperate impulse in the outlaw.

"Don't do it, man," said Silver. "I don't want to murder you with your back turned, but I'll do it sure if you make a move. Get those hands up over your head. That's better, Stew!"

Yet as he spoke, though Stew had thrust his own hands well up over his head, Buck snapped into action.

With one hand he struck at the lantern on the table and sent it crashing the length of the loft room. At the same time he was hurling himself toward the floor, and with his other hand snatching at a revolver.

There was only the tenth of a second for Silver to shoot while the light was still clear enough. He used the first half of that fraction of time to hesitate—in all his life he never before had shot a man through the back. And when he actually fired he was aiming at the hips, or a shade lower.

He knew that the bullet had struck flesh, but that was all he *could* know.

The loft room was in darkness.

From where Buck lay, a revolver began to spit red fire in narrow-throated gusts. And from where Stew stood, another gun was speaking. Those sparks of fire gave weird flickers that were not illumination of the loft, but afforded vague glimpses of what was happening in it.

What they showed was Silver, almost flat on his face, firing in return.

He brought from Stew a yowl of pain with one bullet.

Then footfalls stampeded across the loft floor, straight at him. Silver fired again. The flame from his gun showed him the contorted face of Stew as the man charged madly home. Silver, with the flash of his own shot to guide his next bullet, again fired low. Just at the hip the bullet struck. Stew was flung sidewise, spinning, by the heavy impact of the .45-caliber slug. He struck the floor and skidded along it, then lay still.

Perhaps he was stunned. Perhaps he was merely playing possum, and waiting for a chance to strike a heavy blow for his cause.

A long splinter, ripped from the floor by one of Buck's shots, cracked neatly in two across the head of Silver. He put an answering bullet right into the red flash of Buck's gun and heard the impact of the lead striking flesh, the gasp and sigh of the man.

Silver reached Brender with a leap. He had to fumble a bit to find the right ropes before his knife could cut them, and as he groped he heard Brender choking out vague words that were something between a groan and a song. Those sounds did not need to form syllables, for the first instant that his hand touched his friend, Silver knew that all the peril he had undergone, all the danger that still lay before him, was well braved for the sake of this man.

The shadow of Brender rose beside him and ran toward the ladder, staggering a little, because the pressure of the cords had shut off circulation somewhat and left his legs partially benumbed.

Silver followed. Something in his brain, beating like a metronome, measured off the seconds since the shooting had commenced. The booming echoes of it still seemed to live in the loft of the great barn. Perhaps ten seconds had passed since he opened fire.

And in that time, what had the watchers of Barry Christian done?

Brender was climbing down the ladder. Silver followed. Off to the right, through one of the wide doors of the building, he saw the glance of lantern light that fell on the dark bodies and the pale, gleaming faces of several running men. One of them pointed his hand and fired. Brender loosed his grip on the ladder and dropped to the floor beneath.

Had he been shot through the body?

Silver, swinging out from the ladder, tried a snapshot. The lantern went out; a man yelled sharp and short with pain. Another gun exploded. And now Silver was on the floor of the barn.

All was darkness. Voices and footfalls were retreating from the aisle in which he stood. Brender was not in reaching distance—therefore he must have run on to get to the mare, Chinook. Overhead, the voice of Stew rose like a steam siren, screeching:

"Silver! He's got Brender loose! Help! Silver's got Brender! Stop him! Stop him! Help!"

Every screaming phrase jagged through the brain of Silver like red lightning. Outside the barn, other voices were shouting, and then one pealing cry that rang above the rest:

"The rear door! Guard it!"

Was that the voice of Barry Christian?

Silver was pulling from its stall the mustang he had bridled. He heard the gasp of Brender calling his name. Now he was out in the aisle and astride the little horse, and before him Brender was whipping—a dim shadow— onto the back of Chinook.

"Straight back and through the rear door. Ride like a devil, Rap!" called Silver.

Then Chinook shot down the aisle and almost out of sight. The digging heels of Silver made the mustang lurch in pursuit. It sprawled, skidded, almost fell on the wet flooring. Then, straightening, working desperately, it shot out the doorway with a gathering speed.

Silhouettes of men were rising out of the ground like exhalations. Guns flashed.

A shape ran before Silver, shooting. He tried to fire. The hammer of his gun clicked on an empty chamber. He hurled the gun at the dancing shadow, and it was blotted out against the darkness of the ground.

Well before him raced Chinook, gaining ground with every leap.

"Right, Rap! Right! Right!" wailed Silver.

He saw Brender swing obediently to the right, skirting beyond the houses of the peons. Out of those houses large and small shadows were running like giant wasps out of huge nests.

The shooting had ended. It was a turmoil of voices only that raged behind him, and, mixed with it, the snorting of horses, the beating of racing hoofs.

Beneath him the frightened mustang was doing its best, but he knew that he had caught a slow mover. A dozen animals on that place would surely be able to move almost two feet for its one. So Silver whistled high and shrill and long, a call that Parade had learned to know of old.

Silver looked back, straining his eyes. Behind him he saw swift forms darting through the starlight. There were already half a dozen men in pursuit on fast horses. They called one to another. Above all the others rang one voice.

That was Barry Christian, and that must be Christian's horse which now forged ahead of the others. Chinook drew suddenly back. That was the work of Brender, gallant fool, pulling up his mount to rejoin his friend.

Something shot at Silver from the gloom ahead. He knew the great stride, the inquiring whinny, the lifting head of the stallion, and now Parade swung in at his side, crowding jealously against the mustang.

Silver made that change like a circus rider, at full speed. In an instant he was sitting in the saddle on the back of the stallion. He called, and the cantle of the saddle struck hard against his back as the big horse leaped into full stride.

With his left hand wound into the mane of Parade, he watched the riders of Barry Christian draw back rapidly into obscurity. He caught Chinook and Brender, and heard the Indian yell of triumph from the lips of Rap.

Then, as Silver swung far forward and fitted the bridle over the head of Parade, they left the soft going of the plantation and came out onto the wide, smooth face of the desert, and the rushing wind of the gallop seemed a noise made by wind in the last trees as they swept away into a mound of gloom in the rear.

Other horses were clattering out from the same trees. But what chance had they of overtaking two such flyers? Silver rated Parade to a long, easy lope that kept Chinook laboring to keep up, and gradually the noise of the pursuit melted away, and in the east a pyramid of soft light formed to show where the moon intended to rise.

XV

Christian's Bargain

IN the hotel of Tom Higgins, Buck and Stew lay on their backs in small cots, side by side. Buck grinned at the ceiling with a wider display of white teeth than usual, for pain had puckered his cheeks a little and drawn the lips back. He was very white; his eyes were glassy, as though with fever. Without stirring an eyelid, he lay still and endured pain. Perhaps he would die, perhaps not. The doctor could not tell.

As for Stew, he drew in his breath through his nose and let it out again through his loose lips with a snoring sound. He kept his eyes closed. He would get well, the doctor had said. In the meantime, he either made that snoring sound with his mouth or else used his excess breath to curse steadily.

"Swine!" said Buck in a whisper.

"It was you," answered Stew.

"Me what?"

"You that said it was Christian coming back up the ladder. You that throwed me off guard."

"You heard him speak as good as I did. It sounded like Barry to me," answered Buck. "I hope the soul of you leaks out through the hole he drilled in you."

Big Tom Higgins was pacing up and down the room. He paused now and indicated the two wounded men with a gesture, while he turned to Christian.

"Look at that!" he said. "Good, ain't it? A fine thing for

me to have a coupla thugs like that laid up on my hands if a sheriff or something comes by this way?"

"A few drinks of your bar whisky," said the soft voice of Barry Christian, "will make a whole posse forget the job they're riding on. Don't worry, Tom. But think of the hard cash you'll be paid when this pair is cured."

Higgins sighed. He wet his vast lips and rubbed them off with the back of his hand.

"I ain't arguing," he declared.

Barry Christian rose and smiled on him. Then he stepped between the beds and looked down on the two wounded men.

He said: "You boys will get all that the doctor and Tom Higgins and his men can do for you. When you're cured, you'll get a lay-off and plenty of money to spend on your vacation. You're not being blamed because of what Silver managed to do. It's my fault. Silver being what he is, I ought never to have left Brender's side. There's no worry for you to keep on your mind. When your vacation is over, you'll come back to me. I won't see you again for a good many weeks probably. You'll know where to get in touch with me when you want me. So long!"

Christian turned and called: "Come here, Doc."

Old Doc Shore appeared out of a corner unexpectedly.

"Where you been keeping yourself, old moss-face?" asked Stew.

Doc Shore divided his white beard with his fingers and smiled on the wounded man. Christian laid a hand on the shoulder of the old man.

He said: "Doc, you stay here and run things. Run everything, including what's outside. You're the one who got the message from Lawson to put Silver out, and you planned it well. You called in four big guns to do the trick. One of those guns went wrong, but that wasn't your fault. You couldn't tell that Rap Brender would cross us up. Nobody in my outfit has a better or a faster brain than you have, Doc."

The pink-rimmed eyes of Doc Shore narrowed to slits of fire, so intense was his gratification. He said nothing. Christian waved to the two wounded men in farewell, saying:

"Trust Doc in everything. He'll take care of you boys."

Buck feebly raised a hand in acknowledgment, but Stew

continued to blow out through his lips with the snoring sound.

"Now," said Christian to Tom Higgins, "I want you to tell me where I can find Murcio."

"He's gone to bed," said Higgins.

"Wake him up and send him down to the barroom," said Christian. "I'll be down there helping myself. Hurry it, Tom!"

Higgins hesitated for half a breath, for he was not used to this calm voice of command. Then, as the eye of Christian flicked across his face, he turned in haste and went off with long strides.

Barry Christian went down to the saloon. The door of it being locked, he took a thin splinter of steel from his pocket and worked for an instant, after which the door opened under his hand and he entered. The place was ordinarily illuminated by two big lamps that hung suspended from the ceiling. They were out now, and the only light was from the moon, which sloped in through an eastern window.

Barry Christian stood for a moment inside the door and breathed deeply. It was not the aromatic scent of liquor that he was inhaling, but a far more ethereal fragrance of adventure, for over his mind flashed the pictures of many other rooms that he had seen by the secret light of night.

There was a lantern hanging against the wall. He raised the chimney, scratched a match, and touched the flame to the wick. Then he placed the lantern on the bar and went behind it. There was one bottle of Scotch whisky. He took that and retired to a little table that stood in the corner of the room. The lantern he left on the bar, running its dim fingers across the lines of colored bottles and setting their reflections in the mirror at their back.

He poured out a glass of the whisky, raised it, looked through its ominous amber color at the lantern flame, and then drank it off.

A footfall presently came across the veranda; a hand tried the outer door, opened it, and the round face of Murcio looked inside.

"Come in, Murcio," said Christian.

The Mexican started back and jerked the door almost shut. Then he pushed it open again and entered. He stood with it partially ajar, his hand on the knob as though he were ready for flight.

"Well?" asked Murcio.

"Come in," said Christian.

"I have to go," answered Murcio. "I have to sleep. To-morrow there is a long ride to make."

"Come in," said Christian.

Murcio sighed, closed the door, and advanced unwillingly across the floor.

"I'm drinking Scotch whisky," said Christian. "Go behind the bar and help yourself to anything you want."

"Nothing," said Murcio.

"Then sit down."

The Mexican drew back a chair away from the table and sat down on the edge of it. Christian smiled at him.

"You should not be in bed," said he.

"Why not?"

"You should be riding—you and Santos and the girl, with me."

At this, Murcio lifted both his hands and his shoulders until his fat jowls were compressed.

"She is lost to us, señor!" he said.

"You mean that the little devil has slipped away?" asked Christian.

"No, she is still here. But we cannot take her on. She is lost. The cursed man, Silver, has come. He has seen her. He has seen Brender. They are both free. Nothing will keep them from getting to men of the law. All the desert, all the mountains between this place and Mexico, will soon be swarming with posses. Only the best of fortune can get us through even without her!"

"You think that they're riding straight away to get help. They won't do that. They won't dare," said Christian.

"Dare?" said the Mexican.

"Brender is wanted by the law," said Christian. "He can't show his face to a sheriff."

"There is Silver."

"He won't go to a distance. He'll hang about this place like a hawk over a chicken coop, and with him will be Brender. Ah, there's a romantic lad, Murcio. And the romantic spirit leads us all to do rather foolish things, now and then."

"You mean that they are not riding now to get help? You mean that they are close by us, still about to attempt—no one knows what?"

"They won't come back to try for the girl, I think. Not

to-night," said Christian. "And that's the pity of it. Because if I could put my hands on them again—"

He broke off with a sigh.

"At any rate, Murcio," he said, "you should be in the saddle, you and Santos."

"We start with the first light of the day, or a little before," said Murcio. "But not with the girl."

"If there are only Silver and Brender to think of, why should you be afraid—"

"*Only* Silver and Brender? Only two devils! And we are mere men."

"And you give up the girl—the money?" asked Christian.

Murcio groaned.

"All the fortune!" he muttered. "She will stay in this country. Cursed lawyers will represent her. Soon her possessions will be sold, and my chances are gone!"

"A pity," said Christian. "Now, suppose that I rode with you?"

"You? Why should you do that? There is no hope, señor. We could not carry her through. And I am losing priceless hours of sleep in vain. If we ride off with her, then either a thousand posses will stop us, or else—"

"If we ride off with her and are not followed at heel," said Christian, "I tell you, Murcio, that I can find twenty places in the mountains to the south where we'll never be found until the hunt dies down. Then we can ride on at leisure."

"Are you sure?" said Murcio.

"But we'll be followed by the pair of them," went on Christian. "You can be sure of that. Good men, Murcio, don't allow a poor young persecuted girl to be swept away by villains like us."

He laughed soundlessly. Murcio shuddered as though the whisper broke like icy waves on his heart.

"They will be lingering close by," said Christian. "You can be sure of that."

"And if they are near, is it true that they have horses which eagles can hardly catch?" groaned Murcio.

"They have two good horses," agreed Christian. "There is a golden chestnut stallion that Silver rides, and for the sake of that horse I think I would give up two fortunes like that of this girl. But there is a way in which we can leave even the stallion and his rider behind."

"Tell me," said Murcio.

"Of course I'll tell you," said the genial Christian. "It happens that I have friends scattered here and there. For what is a man's life if it be naked of friendships, Murcio?"

"Go to the point! Go to the point!" groaned Murcio. "Friendships—yes, yes! I admit anything you want in the way of moralizing. But tell me how we can be snatched out of the hands of these two fiends?"

"In several ways, Murcio. We might draw them on into the desert and then turn back and fight them. I haven't your awe of them, quite. But better still, and more easily done, I'll send a man out from this place to ride far ahead of us. He will find, every fifty miles or so, certain friends of mine of whom I've been speaking. From each of them he'll ask half a dozen good, tough mustangs. And so we'll gallop along in relays, with fresh horses everyday. You understand? Not even that golden stallion will be able to keep up with us. In three days it will be worn out and fall back from a trot to a stagger. And the rest of us will go happily on!"

Murcio sprang to his feet. "It can be done!" he cried. "I feel it—and I see the happy ending. It *can* be done!"

"There's the price to agree on," said Christian. "And then to horse and away, amigo."

"Ah, the price! Yes, yes, the price!" groaned Murcio.

He slumped back into his chair and stared gloomily toward Christian.

"What will the whole estate come to?" asked Christian.

"Oh, it's a handsome thing," said Murico. "Perhaps two, perhaps even three hundred thousand dollars."

"In cattle, eh?" said Christian.

"Yes, and in other things."

"Three hundred in cattle, and then there's the matter of the good timberland down there in Central America, in San Nicador, say? That would be another two or three hundred thousand?"

"Not half so much!" exclaimed Murcio. "Who told you—"

"Besides," said Christian, "the items you have forgotten, such as stocks and bonds, here and there, and a number of little odds and ends of real estate."

Murcio was silent for a moment. Then he burst out: "Where did you learn all of these things?"

"She has said two words, and you have said two, and

Santos has said a dozen more," said Christian. "It isn't hard for a good artist to paint a portrait after he's had even a glimpse of his subject. And for my services, Murcio, I'll take from you your note dated three months hence, for two hundred thousand dollars."

"Two hundred—señor! Two hundred thousand, did you say?"

"Listen, my dear Murcio," said Christian. "You won't deny me the right to be a thrifty man and to make a thrifty bargain, will you? Next to godliness, isn't thrift the most admirable virtue? And now I am giving you the chance to lay your hands on twice as much as I ask from you. I have drawn up the litlte paper here. Walk over to the bar and sign it, if you please."

"Do you think that we can beggar her?" said Murcio, as a last resort. "Do you think that we can rob her shamelessly of her last penny?"

"With your law courts and with your cleverness, yes," said Christian. "And besides, it will be a good thing. What is more touching, what is more appealing than innocence and beauty cast penniless into this harsh world?"

XVI

Desert March

THEY went out of the Higgins oasis as a party of five, with ten horses. The spare horses were loaded with waterskins, after the Mexican fashion of carrying the liquid across the desert, and it was estimated that they had enough water to last them for three days of hot marching.

They started at a dogtrot, for a slow beginning is apt to make a strong ending. It was the hope of Barry Christian that he would be able to shake off all pursuit before the torrid heat of that desert march had ended. He could have headed due south. He chose, instead, to take a straight line southwest across the most terrible of the alkali flats. With

Silver and Brender there could not possibly be such provision against thirst, and they had but one horse apiece.

With Christian traveled the girl, of course, and Murcio, also big Alonso Santos, on whose bulk and poundage Christian cast a doubtful eye more than once, and finally one of Christian's most trusted men, "Blondy." He was almost an albino and therefore he deserved his name. Lean and desert-dried, weightless in body, quick as a snake to strike and deadly as a snake in his effects, Blondy was a perfect tool in the hand of Christian. There was nothing in the world that he loved and there was only one thing in the world that he feared—Christian himself. When Blondy's white eyelids were lowered, there was in his face no more expression than in a stone. But when he looked suddenly up, as was his way, one could occasionally see a little reddish-yellow flame wavering in his eyes. That fire, burning dim or bright, was never entirely absent.

They jogged the horses steadily forward, Blondy first, as being the one best acquainted with the desert of this section, then the girl on a good pinto mustang, a rope running from the neck of the pony to the pommel of Blondy's saddle. Next came Murcio, then Santos, and last of all, a good bit behind so that he would be out of the dust, rode Christian in the post of honor.

It was the post of honor because it was the place of danger, and it was his duty to scan the horizon behind them with his keen eyes, continually.

The moon was very bright and clear. The windless night had left the air undisturbed by dust, comparatively, and the stars were unusually keen points of brilliance. Yet for all this clarity of the atmosphere, Christian spotted nothing suspicious behind them.

As morning approached, a thrill of hope began to grow in him that perhaps there would be no clash with Silver whatever and that that pursuer would never find their traces leading away from the oasis. The dawn came on. The banded color about the horizon grew from ochre to crimson, to gold, and then all color ended as the white sun slid above the sky line and instantly began to burn them to the bone.

They paused, ate a breakfast of raisins and hardtack, and changed the saddles to the backs of the mustangs that had been carrying the lighter waterskins. After that, they went on again. And Barry Christian came up to ride at the side of the girl for a few moments.

The sun was very strong and keen by this time, and every face in the party was flushed, except the face of Christian. He, instead, was as pale as ever—not chalky-white, as usual, but a more translucent clarity of skin.

He looked over Rosa Cardigan with a shrewdly appraising eye and took note of her erectness in the saddle and the brightness of her eye.

"I see," said Christian. "All of this trouble and all of this pother, when the dear girl wanted nothing, really, except to kill homesickness by getting back to her native land. Why else should you be shining and glowing like this, Rosa Cardigan?"

She was still half smiling, as she glanced at him, though he could see that the smile had nothing to do with him.

"I'm happy because I see the end of it," she said.

"What end?" he asked her.

She made a quick gesture, as though the thing were too obvious to call for more explanation.

"You help them take me back to Mexico. Once there, I can be legally robbed. Once robbed, I'll be free entirely. And *then* I can come back!"

"Ah," said Christian. "To Brender? Then you come back to him?"

"I do," she said.

"Does he know that?"

"No. He ought to know it, but he doesn't."

"An outlaw?" said Christian. "My poor girl, what a sad future for you—to be married to an outlaw!"

She merely laughed.

"Now I should think," said Christian, "that you'd cast an eye on the hero of the two, the great Silver, the terrible man. Why not?"

She amazed him by saying: "Perhaps I would. But I found Rap Brender first. And there's no space left in me. Besides, Silver is too grim. I think of him still, half smiling, and his step gliding, and the gray marks above his temples, like horns. I'd be afraid of him—as you are!"

"Yes," said Christian, with a sudden need for confession of the latent terror within him, "I'm afraid of him. Otherwise it would not be so important that he must die. We've shaken him off now. He'll not interfere again, I imagine. And when I come back from Mexico—"

He opened his hand, then closed the fingers slowly together. And she watched him, fascinated, well understanding that in his thought he was crushing out a human life.

"And you wouldn't turn back if he followed?" she asked. "You wouldn't turn back to—to crush him?"

"Blondy and I," said Christian in his gentle voice, "are the escort of a rich fleet of merchant ships. Of course we won't risk a fight that we can run from. Not until the cargoes are safely in some harbor."

Her glance wandered away from him and far to the side and the rear where a small cloud of dust was rising; it might have been lifted by a whirl in the dead air of the desert. No, it was persisting.

Barry Christian followed the direction of her eyes. He saw that continuing little puff of dust, stopped his horse, and drawing out a pair of field glasses, stared long. The four went on from him.

He remained behind with the studious glass fixed on the target. He saw it move. He saw the head of the dust cloud rolling. And then, beneath it, he made out two small forms. As his gaze focused more carefully, he could distinguish the sheen of one of the horses, like metal, like gold, in fact.

That was enough for Christian. He came up at a gallop and joined the others.

"Freshen up this pace," he said. "Let's have a real trot. Break it for a lope, when your bones begin to rattle loose. But keep to the trot as long as you can. We may need everything that we can get out of these horses. Because Brender and Silver are coming up with us. There they are, over yonder. If they're in striking distance by nightfall, something is likely to happen to us."

So the rate of travel was raised. The cracking trot shook the riders from head to foot. The saddles creaked and groaned. The horses began to blacken and then to drip with sweat. Perspiration soaked through the shirts and the coats of the riders and left dark stains, rimmed around with white edgings of salt. Before them the desert was covered with dim reddish haze that blurred all things but gave no shelter against the sun. And there was no shade. The greasewood stretched, here and there, like a faint smoke near the ground. The mesquite bushes held up the edges of their leaves to cleave the terrible blaze of the sun. There was no wind to cool the body or help breathing. They were in a moving caldron. The dust they raised was the steam of the pot. And they cooked as the mustangs trotted on, jolting the breath from their bodies.

It was forced march. Now and then they halted, and the dust rose slowly, then began to settle again. Sweat continued to run on the horses, but the moisture on the outer hair disappeared almost at once, and the animals turned gray with salt. The dry air and the fierceness of the sun sucked at the very forces of the body. It seemed to be drawing up the life through the throat. It was a time when they could have ridden with a canteen in the hand, constantly sipping but never keeping very far ahead of the drain of the heat and the dryness.

Yet none of them attempted large inroads on the water supply. Their own needs for water were small compared with their need of life itself. And if the little dust cloud in the rear were able to come up with them, bullets would begin to sing.

Blondy could stand the thing no longer. He called to his chief and when Christian came up, exclaimed:

"There's four males here, and they're running away from two gents that are all alone!"

He glared fiercely at Christian, but his leader merely smiled.

"Murcio can use a gun; Santos is an excellent shot," said Christian. "And they both will fight when the need comes. But the need doesn't come until we've burned up the horseflesh."

"I don't sort of foller that," commented Blondy.

"When there's long-range shooting, anything is likely to happen," said Christian. "If a lucky shot hits me, I'm out. It won't need killing. Any sort of a wound will make the fellow that's hit drop out of the race. If a bullet snags you, the same thing happens. That's all. And if one of us goes down, the two Mexicans are likely to lose heart. They're likely to scatter to either side and leave the sole survivor carrying on—with the girl on his hands. Does that picture appeal to you?"

"I never knew you to turn your back on no two gents before," said Blondy grimly.

"Ah, Blondy," said Christian, "the fact is that you never saw me convoying merchandise across a desert before!"

Blondy was silenced. He turned his eyes toward the north, where the feet of the mountains were lost behind the mist, but their blue shoulders and their pale heads were clear against the sky. He looked south and saw nothing but the dancing heat waves that rose from the surface of the plain. And turning, he stared straight into the face of the girl.

She was the least exhausted of the troop; she actually rode with a faint smile that was rather in her eyes than on her lips.

"There's Injun blood in her," commented Blondy to himself.

They made a dry camp and stayed in it for four hours, with two men constantly on guard. Then they marched on. In the clear morning light they saw the southern mountains, many a bitter march away from them, but as the day increased, the mountains turned into sky phantoms and then disappeared entirely. And now the horses began to stumble.

Blondy, whose dry body weighed no more than that of a boy, was given the freshest horse in the party and sent on ahead. By noon he was waiting with a relay of horses and an old brown veteran of a desert rat who took over the ten mustangs of the party and led them off toward his dry ranch. And those fresh mounts put new vigor into the riders. Only Murcio could no longer endure the ceaseless racking of the trot. He either walked or loped his mustang.

The next day they repeated that performance, Blondy again riding off in advance, on the strongest horse, and appearing once more with fresh horses.

Now they could see the southern mountains clearly, by day and by night, and though there were many bitter leagues to be covered, Murcio and Santos were highly optimistic. Beyond the mountains and their foaming creeks they would find the river, and beyond the river lay Mexico. And into Mexico the pursuers would hardly dare to pass, or if they did, it would then be safe for Christian to turn back and strike them.

And still, every day, sooner or later into the view of the fugitives drew that small attendant cloud of dust. There could not be changes of horses for Silver and Brender, and yet they continued to keep near! They could not come quite up with the pursued and yet they could not be shaken off. The thing seemed a marvel.

Christian dropped back into rifle range one day, and examined the pursuit carefully with his field glasses. Then he came back to explain the mystery of the manner in which that pair, without a change of horses, had been able to keep up with the relayed flight of the group. For Christian had seen the two running on foot, driving tirelessly forward. He had seen the horses following behind, Chinook without a burden and the stallion carrying both saddles. His strength was greater, and the power of the mare was being conserved. So Silver and Brender must have passed hour after hour, each day, perhaps running on through the worst of the heat.

That was why they were able to bring up their chase a little nearer each day!

When Christian made that report, the two Mexicans looked suddenly askance at one another. They were brave enough, but it seemed now that the two who hunted them were a great deal more than human. The Mexicans looked down at the stony face of the desert. It was almost more than flesh could endure to sit the saddles through the long hours of the day, to say nothing of running on foot.

"They'll be losing their spare fat," said Christian cheerfully to the girl.

But she smiled no longer.

"They *will* catch up," she said.

"And then?" asked Christian.

"And then they'll be murdered!" said the girl. "Are you only drawing out their misery? Are you only letting them torture themselves with hope so that you can laugh at them all these days? And then in the end you'll crush them!"

He caught quickly at the air with his hand.

"Like flies!" said Christian softly.

XVII

The Pursuers

IN the heat of midday Silver covered the ground with a long swinging stride. He ran like an Indian, his body straight above the hips, his chin down, his legs moving with a tireless rhythm and the heel striking the ground a little before the toes. On his feet were improvised sandals with soles made of the saddle flaps. The stallion followed at his heels, a gaunt, rib-staring mockery of the sleek beauty that had left the oasis of Tom Higgins. A step or two back ran Rap Brender, leading Chinook. She was so spent that she had been dragging her feet for the last twenty-four hours and the hoofs were being beveled at the toes.

As for Silvertip, every ounce of fat was gone from his sinews. The skin of his face was hard-drawn. There was a hollow at the base of his throat, and the breastbone thrust out prominently. But there was still strength in him, as in the stallion. They were spent but they were not beaten.

Then, although he heard nothing, he was aware that something had happened behind him. He glanced back and saw Brender lying face down in the sand.

Silver returned. He had been half afraid of this during all the last day but had refused to let his fear get up into his brain. He had locked it back behind his set teeth.

Now he lifted the loose body and laid it on its back in the shelter of the mare.

She stood with hanging head and ears flopped forward, as though she were listening to a voice that rose out of the ground.

Brender was unconscious. His face was still crimson in places from the terrible effort of the run, but white like that of frostbite was all about his mouth and was rapidly spreading into his cheeks. His eyes were sunk into shadows. His face had wasted as though a fever had been burning in him constantly.

Silver took from his saddle a canteen wrapped in sacking. He sat cross-legged, took Brender's head in the crook of his arm, and forced the mouth open. It resisted with a shuddering effort, then hung loose. He poured in a swallow of water, watched it go down the skinny throat, and poured in more. He began to drop that priceless liquid in small splashes on the forehead and throat of the senseless body.

At last Brender opened his eyes and tried to sit up. Silver pressed him back into a recumbent position.

"I sort of stumbled," said Brender. "I sort of stumbled and I must have banged my head on the ground."

Silver wiped away from the face of his friend the dust that had turned to streaks of mud. Brender was still pale, but not the same deadly white. He was breathing more deeply; his heart no longer fluttered. In his throat a regular though rapid pulse was visible.

"You just went out; that's all," said Silver. "Why didn't you tell me that you were out on your feet?"

Brender blinked at the sternness of that voice and answered:

"Chinook couldn't carry me ten miles. There was no good asking her to."

"We've got to get fresh horses," said Silver. "We've got to get *one* at least. They've been beating us with the relays. To-morrow they'll be able to pull right away from us. They'll get to the mountains. We can never catch 'em there. They'll be over the river and then into Mexico—and we're done for. We've got to get fresh horses, because to-morrow is the great day. Rap, start thinking. Make your head clear. Somewhere this side of the settlements there's a place where you can find a horse. Christian keeps finding them for his whole gang."

"He knows the dry farmers," said Brender. "He's bought them up. They're his friends. And besides, I don't know where they're located. There's only one place inside of ten miles of this spot where we could get horses, and that place is no good."

"What place?" asked Silver.

"It's no good. You couldn't get anything out of Crosseyed Harry Trench and his vaqueros. He'd fill you full of lead. He doesn't ask questions. When a stranger comes along, he just starts shooting and his Mexicans do the same thing. You couldn't get horses from him. Not even Christian would try that place. I've heard Stew and the rest say so. Not even Christian with a gang behind him would try to get anything from that Cross-eyed Harry Trench."

"Where's his place?"

"Right yonder, toward that mesa. Wait a minute. Hold on, Silver. Don't be a fool. You can't get anything from Cross-eyed Harry."

Silver stood up.

"You do what you can," he said. "Take my advice and stay here. Stay put. But if you have to keep going, don't follow me. Ride straight on down the line that Christian and the rest are taking. I'm going to get some horses from Harry Trench and I'll join you later on."

He swung onto the back of Parade. Brender, raised to his feet with a sudden horror, began to cry out in protest, but Parade was already swinging away at a long gallop, and the rider pretended to hear nothing from behind.

It was by no means ten miles, in fact, before Silver came in sight of the little dobe house. It was so small that it was lost to view until one was fairly close, and at about the same time that Silver spotted it, he saw a man walk out of the black shadow of the doorway and stand in the sun with a rifle in his hands.

That would be "Cross-eyed Harry," perhaps, ready to act as a reception committee to strangers!

Silver rode the stallion into a steep-sided draw that opened at the left and ran on in the general direction of the house. Where the bank of the draw became shallower, so that it would not shelter horse and rider from the eye, Silver dismounted, tied the reins over the pommel of the saddle, and with a whisper commanded Parade to stand still. Then he went on foot and then on hands and knees down the draw.

At last he could see the flat roof of the hut near by.

The instant he stood up, a rifle bullet kissed the air beside his head. He saw Cross-eyed Harry standing huge and formidable, long hair sweeping down to his shoulders, his rifle leveled; murder his intention.

Silver put a bullet through the right shoulder of the giant. It merely clipped the outer flesh, but it cut enough nerves to make the rifle sag. And Cross-eyed Harry took the gun under his left arm as Silver raced in. In the vast grasp of Trench that heavy rifle was hardly more than a revolver for an ordinary man. He had swung the gun across and brought it to a level, to use it like a pistol, when Silver reached him. Silver's hard fist might have done the trick, but he could take no chances with the brute. He hammered the long barrel of his Colt along the jaw of Trench and watched the bulk of the man topple sidewise.

Silver took from the senseless hand the rifle, a pair of revolvers from hip holsters, and a great hunting knife from the inside belt.

He stepped into the hut.

There was a bit of a primus stove that had soaked the entire interior with a layer of soot. A cot stood in a corner; some traps hung from the wall. Moldering, ancient garments hung from pegs. The floor was the bare earth. A saddle, also, was on the wall, with a strong Mexican rawhide lariat hanging from it.

Silver took down the saddle and stepped through the door of the hut. Cross-eyed Harry Trench was sitting up, bracing himself on his hands, regarding Silver with deathless hate out of his unfocused eyes.

"Afterwards," said Silver, "I'm coming back this way. I'm giving you your chance now. But I'm coming back. And when I come, you're going to wave a hat at me, not a gun. You hear? You're going to cook food and coffee. You're going to act like a human, not like a wolf. Or otherwise, I'm going to plant you in your front yard."

"You're a greaser!" said Cross-eyed Harry. "Ain't that what you are? A greaser?" He looked closely into the sun-darkened face of Silver.

"I'm Americano," said Silver.

The other sighed and nodded. "That's better," he said. "I knew that I'd have to get mine, one of these days. I dunno that I care so much, seeing you ain't a greaser! Whatcha want?"

"A horse, a canteen of water, some barley or oats, some hardtack and jerked beef, or anything you've got, like that."

"Wait a minute," said Trench. "Seeing that you can help yourself, lemme give you a hand and show you where things lay."

Fortune had smiled on Christian and his friends from

the start; now it betrayed them in the time of greatest need, for Blondy, who had been sent ahead to bring in the fourth relay of horses, appeared on the line of march, but alone, and with his horse very exhausted from the rapid pace to which he had forced it. His report was simply that where the ranch house to which he was sent had once stood there was now only a black smudge across the ground, and on the sun-burned range around it, there was not a sign of either horse or beef. The outfit had been burned out and had moved on, which was not very strange, for on the edge of the naked desert the grazing was always very poor.

At the same time that Blondy appeared with this bad news, the thin dust cloud which meant the pursuit heaved again on the northeastern horizon and began to close in with startling speed.

That was not all. For the girl, who had endured the ride better than any of the men except the great Christian himself—for his lean frame seemed incapable of fatigue—had showed signs of depression that morning for the first time; by noon her face was flushed, her eyes dim, and by the mid-afternoon she was reeling in the saddle, clinging to the pommel with both hands, and looking about her in the delirium of a high fever.

Christian, studying the rapid approach of the dust cloud with his field glasses, made out not two figures, but four, and presently could distinguish a pair of horses mounted and a pair on the lead.

He broke into a strange cry to Blondy: "He's found remounts! He has fresh horses, Blondy!"

"It ain't likely. It ain't possible," said Blondy. "There ain't any place where he could 'a' got 'em, except from Cross-eyed Harry."

"He's persuaded Harry Trench to mount him, at any rate," said Christian, "and that's one of the wonders of this world. Harry Trench? I'd as soon try to persuade a Bengal tiger!"

"If he got horses there," said Blondy confidently, "the gent that he persuaded was a dead man, and Silver did the killing. You can lay to that! Ride close to the girl's hoss, chief. She's going to fall on her head in a minute."

Christian accepted that advice and presently was at the side of Rosa. Her head rolled from side to side as though all strength had gone from her neck.

There was one cheering prospect for the fugitives. That was the nearness of the mountains. All that day they had loomed clearly before the eye as they rode south, printed in detail of shining rocks, and trees, and the thin, hairlike flash of a creek now and then running down the slopes; all the summits were lost in dense cloud.

Now the heights were so close that at last the distance to the foothills could be estimated exactly, and the deep shadows of the ravines promised them shelter at last from the sun. That was why they pushed on more cheerfully, though now even to the naked eye the four forms on the horizon were clear, with the dust cloud rising and trailing behind.

It seemed for a time that Silver and Brender might actually close to good rifle range before the foothills were reached, but with whip and spur the four scourged the last effort out of their mustangs and entered the first long ravine well in the lead. Above them mounted a dimly winding trail which they followed for some time and at last entered a narrow ravine where the shadow sloping from the west covered them with coolness, like flowing water. Occasional breezes, also, now dipped into the hollows. Overhead, the cloud masses streamed far out into the sky, wind-whipped, before the rain mists were dissipated in the brilliance of the sun. It was apparent that a furious storm was blowing from the south and west on the farther side of the mountains.

Well down the ravine, they came to a narrow gap beyond which a second valley opened, with a rougher floor and a steeper rise.

"Go on!" said Blondy to Christian. "Go on with the loot. But I've rode long enough on the run. I'm going to take a berth here behind one of these rocks and plaster those two gents as they go by. It ain't going to be hard. It's the sort of a thing that we'd ought to 'a' done long before."

"Do as you please," said Christian. "but I'll warn you of this—that all the weariness in the world won't make the eye of Silver a whit less keen. He'll see anything that a hawk could notice."

"Yeah?" growled Blondy, his eyes blazing. "He's human: that's all that he is! You can lay to it that he ain't any more'n human. So long. I'll be seeing you later!"

He turned aside from the rest, at that, and they toiled

steadily up and up the slope, taking the easier grades but always finding such sharp angles that it was necessary to dismount every one except the girl and struggle up on foot. The wind was growing stronger as the sun declined in the west, and now occasional strong gusts struck at them with the cold of snow. And when the billowing darkness of the storm lifted a little, here and there, they could see far up the summits the white sheets of the snow and the ice. They would be inside the storm fog before long, and with the slippery snow beneath their feet. The girl was already shuddering at every touch of the wind, though Christian had drawn his slicker about her shoulders.

So they came out on a projecting shoulder of the mountain from which they could look straight down into the ravine from which they had risen in so many zigzags. Through the crystal purity of the air they were able to see the small form of Blondy stretched out on the top of a great boulder, lying at ease with his rifle at his shoulder; his mustang had been tied in a clump of brush near by.

Murcio began to beat his hands together softly, forgetful that no sound he could make would reach to the ears of any one at that distance below.

"There!" he said. "Blondy has them. He'll bag them both, like two geese. You see, Santos? You see how the fools ride straight into the mouth of the danger?"

Thunder sounded high up among the mountain peaks, as though to give an accent to the words of the Mexican. Santos, peering carefully over the edge of the abyss, began to laugh a little breathlessly. He had grown thin during the long pursuit. Some of his dignity had left him, and now that his face was unfleshed, the size of his nose made him look like a bird of prey.

"They're gone," said Santos. "They can't escape from him, now that they're at such close range. Look at that, Señor Christian, and tell me!"

Christian looked back first at the girl. She was swaying in the saddle though the horse stood still, and in her face there was the blindness of one who is enthralled and totally occupied by nothing except physical suffering.

He squinted at her, weighing the amount of strength that remained to her. Then he looked down at the picture beneath. Right up to the little rough ravine rode Brender and Silver. Behind them Chinook and the golden stallion were on the lead.

"It's true!" exclaimed Christian. "He has them now. He can't miss Silver at the first shot, and he'll get Brender before he can turn and run! They're lost! They're gone!"

He shouted the words loudly, in exultation.

Then the noise died out. Murcio looked with wonder toward Christian and Santos, as though seeking for an explanation which neither of them could offer. For the two riders were now almost on top of the rock. Now they were abreast of it—and yet Blondy continued to aim the rifle down the canyon!

Here Silver swung to the left and reaching over the top of the rock, calmly took the rifle from Blondy, whose body now rolled loosely over on its back!

"Dead!" exclaimed Christian. Then he added in his usual voice of softness: "Ah, there was something in what I told him! That Silver would see whatever a hawk could see. As I said, so he did. Perhaps even from a distance he saw the glint of sunshine on the muzzle of the rifle, and his own rifle was instantly out of its holster—a snapshot from a distance and a bullet through the brain of Blondy! No wonder he lies there so still! Ah, well, that is the way it happens with the rash! One false step destroys them utterly.

"But we, my friends, have now learned something at Blondy's cost. We know how one pays by exposing so much as a bright coat button to a marksman like Silver! What a hand, what an eye, what a magnificent and fearless creature, gentlemen—pushing into the mountains on our trail, though he knows that we might be hidden in force behind any of a thousand rocks or buried in any of the thousand patches of brush!"

"We might be, but we won't," Murcio said abruptly. It's all very well for a fool like Blondy to give us the proof, but after we have it, we know that life is better than a lot of money and a grave. We're going to keep straight on till we're in Mexico!"

"We are!" agreed Santos. "If she had six million dollars instead of six hundred thousand, we'd still head straight on for Mexico. If we can save her and the money by marching, very well. But as for fighting a devil who shoots by instinct and cannot miss—that, Señor Christian, would be foolish."

"Very well," said Christian calmly. "We shall keep on marching, as you suggest, and when it comes to the matter of fighting, then we'll see. Only, my friends, *I* shall not give up the game until I've been forced to it. It's a matter of principle. Merely a matter of business principle. I must keep the record of the man who never fails. Can I afford to have one black mark against me?"

For the moment, Barry Christian believed this. His hatred of Jim Silver, born of the fact that Silver was the only man who had ever foiled him, had even put black marks against him, was so rampant that the twisted mind failed to remember. What was past, was past, Christian to himself was invincible; only by that belief could he hope to prevail against his archenemy.

XVIII

The Storm

TEN minutes later, they had turned into a pass that pointed through the heart of the mountains. Down that cleft through the range, like water along an immense flume, the storm wind poured and threatened to sweep them from their feet. It was as though the desert sun had lightened them until they were paper figures that the wind could lift and toss away. Such was the fluid weight of that blast that even the horses were again and again stopped or staggered by it.

And the girl was kept in the saddle only by the arm of Christian, who was constantly beside her.

Still they climbed. The ground turned white and slippery beneath them, and all progress was doubly difficult. The breath of the storm was constantly around them, thick as steam, with leaping ghosts and shrieking devils running through it.

The whole whirling mist became a dim conflagration at

the time of sunset, when the ardent colors, rose and golden, turned the storm fog to rolling fire.

Murcio came close to Christian.

"We can't go on," he declared. "Santos is almost ready to fall. So am I!"

"Fall then, my friend," said Christian. "The snow will soon bury you!"

"We must turn back," yelled Murcio, waving both arms. "Señor Christian, what good is the girl to you unless you know how to draw the money away from her? And I am the only one who can do that. Besides, she's dying! See her face! She's turning blue. She'd fall to the ground except for your help!"

Christian turned his head and stared for an instant at the swaying body of Rosa. Then he nodded.

"It's true," he said. "We can't take her on into this gale. Besides, we've almost come to the river. And I know a place where we can spend the night as safely, Murcio, as though we were in Mexico City! You and Santos follow and hold up the girl. I'll go ahead on foot. We have to turn right off the pass. But don't worry. I know the way. Follow me closely. I know these mountains so well, amigo, that I could walk through them with my eyes blindfolded."

He took the lead accordingly and, turning to the right between the roots of two tall peaks, moved around the side of the left-hand summit right into the fiercest teeth of the wind. It was now almost dark. The storm cloud was so dense as the twilight failed that it was a blindfold pressed close to the eyes. They had to call to one another to make sure that they were in touch, and at last Christian turned straight in through tall brush that grew on a slight shoulder of the mountain.

He found a dead bush, tore it up, beat the water from the leaves, and presently kindled the branches. Then he held up that torch, half flaming and half streaming smoke, and led the way through a cleft hardly three feet wide. It opened into a winding cavern that gained a good deal in width at once and presently rose to such a height that the top of the split was lost to that feeble light. It seemed that the crevice extended to the top of the peak.

For a good fifty feet Christian went on, until he had reached the point of the greatest width. There he paused.

"Take charge of the girl, Murcio," he said. "Get her between blankets, Santos, unlimber the cooking pans. We can eat here. I'll rustle wood. We'll spend a snug night and when the wind's blown out, we'll go down and ford the river. Anything easier than that?"

By the time the fire was lighted and the fume of bacon and the steam of fragrant coffee was in the air, it seemed in fact that a pleasanter place could hardly be found. After the heat of the desert the sudden cold had bitten them all to the bone, but now they had the fire to warm them and the scent of cookery, and above all there was shelter from the wind. Now and then the storm put its lips to the mouth of the cave and thundered through it as through a vast horn, but as a rule the yelling of the wind was far away.

A great quantity of the brush had been carried in. Some of it had been used for the building of beds on the tops of which the blankets could be spread. More was reserved for fuel. For water they had lumps of snow brought in from the mountainside. There were only two sources of anxiety—could Silver manage to follow the trail they had left, through the darkness, and was the girl seriously ill?

Christian answered both questions in his soft voice.

He bared an arm to the elbow and put the naked flesh against the forehead of the girl.

"Over a hundred," he said presently. "But not a great deal more. Food and rest from the sun will help her. In a few hours she'll be as sound as can be. That's what I hope at least. She's tough. We've had a chance to see that. She's lost hardly five pounds on the trip, and the rest of us are scarecrows. About Silver—well, I suppose that through the storm and the darkness only one man in ten thousand would even attempt to follow a trail. Let's say that he's the one man in ten thousand. But in addition to the darkness, he'll find that the blowing snow has filled most of the tracks. The cold will begin to freeze them, too. I think that Brender will not be able to hold up, no matter what strength there may be in Silver. Silver will be halted by Brender's weakness. Trust my word when I say that the girl means nothing to Silver, compared with the welfare of his friend."

He laughed his silent laugh. Then he added:

"For in Señor Silver, my dear friends, we meet the man of the gentle heart which feareth not, the noble soul which quaileth not, and whose love surpasseth the love of man for woman!"

In the bleak grip of the wind, Silver and Brender had actually gained the throat of the pass down which the others had proceeded before them. Flurries of snow or heavy-handed hail beat at them; the wind itself was a hand that thrust into their mouths and made straining pockets of their cheeks when they strove to speak. But still they went on, Silver on foot, Brender in the saddle on the golden stallion, fallen far forward so that his head and shoulders could break the force of the wind and keep it from cutting like a sword through his weakened body.

The other three horses had been abandoned at the mouth of the pass. Chinook was very badly done in. The two mustangs they had secured from Cross-eyed Harry Trench had been ridden out in the last strain of crossing the desert and of staggering up the exhausting face of the mountains. Only Parade remained capable of action. And at last Silver had helped the sinking body of Brender into the saddle on the stallion. It was not easy to keep him there. Parade could hardly be held from bucking the weight of the stranger from the saddle. It was only the hand and the voice and the eye of his master that kept the great stallion from beginning to rear and plunge.

But Silver would not give up the quest. And as long as he went on, Brender would not turn back.

Yet it seemed worse than looking for a needle in a haystack. Now and again, sitting on the ground with legs spread out, Silver would light a match and scan the center of the trail.

That feeble flicker of light would show to Brender the bare head, the starved face of his friend, and the body of Silver wrapped in a saddle blanket as in a cloak, and then the tattered cotton trousers, and the naked shanks, looking absurdly weak and thin, and the blood-stained sandals on the feet.

To Silver, the light was showing no more than the trail itself and the possible imprint of hoofs or of boots. Now and again, when the light showed nothing but drifted snow, with his freezing fingers he could brush off the top of the drift and so find the depressions which the marching feet had left.

And so he would be up and on again.

Sometimes the voice of Brender cried out to him that it was madness and death for them both, but Silver went on,

Then, after long labor, the storm melted out of the sky.

In an hour the zenith was clear, and a half moon, standing up in the east, showed them a world of dazzling white summits set against a sky of dark-gray, pointed with the glistening stars.

Brender, wonderfully cheered, seemed to recover half of his lost strength the instant that the wind no longer tore at him.

He climbed down from the saddle and joined Silver in the hunt for a sign.

But not a trace of a track could be found.

They had come too far, and the fugitives must have turned off the course at some point.

So they went back, halting every hundred yards or so to hunt for the impressions of hoofs and feet, until at last they picked up the trail again at a point where a sort of cross pass cut into the main one.

Here they worked on hands and knees, patiently. The cold had increased strangely with the fall of the wind. If it did not bite so deep, it paralyzed the hands and the feet more quickly. They had to stop every moment to stamp and beat their hands together.

But search as they might, they could not find the point at which the sign recommenced. Perhaps the wind had filled all the tracks with a more compacted snow. Perhaps the beating of a flurry of hail had here jammed the snow together into a solid mass.

Silver said at last, and though his voice was quiet, it sounded deep and preternaturally loud in the uncanny silence of that high, white world: "Rap, we'll have to split here. It may be that they've turned off up this canyon—or down it. Or it may be that they've gone a long distance ahead before they turned. Or, for that matter, they may have gone all the way through the pass. But this is where the sign stops, and we'll have to try here to pick up the sign. You turn to the left there. I'll go to the right between the roots of these two mountains. If you find any sign, come back and wait for me here. If I find any sign, I'll come back and wait for you."

He took the ice-cold hand of Brender. Under the white moon each man looked into the drawn, dark face of the other. Then they parted in silence, and the stallion followed closely behind the footsteps of Silver. He found himself rounding the steep side of the mountain on his own left, presently, for a little gorge opened between this and the adjoining mountain. He came out on a narrow shoulder. Looking down from it, he saw the lofty walls of a canyon, and in the bottom, around one bend, the moon looked in on the rush of a river.

For a moment, in spite of his quest and in spite of the cold, Silver paused there and let the beauty of the place freeze into his soul. And he heard a voice come up to him out of the vast distance, like a tremor running up from the earth into his body. It came from the wide bend where the water frothed white in a cataract.

He swung around to continue on his way, when another voice came to him out of the heart of the rocky mountain—and the sound was that of human laughter!

Something more than cold helped to freeze him now. Then he turned and walked straight into the tall brush that grew here all along the steep. A faint aroma of cookery reached him, and half his fear dissolved at a stroke. If ghosts cooked bacon, he wanted to meet the spirits of that ilk!

Then he found the cleft in the wall of the mountain. It was merely a grayness of light in the solid blackness, a hint rather than an actual gleam of radiance that caught his eye, but it was enough to lead him one step into the gloom.

Then voices and footsteps came toward him. He drew rapidly back. The stallion, at a gesture from the master, turned into a shrinking, cat-like monster, stealing back into the brush. And there, shrouded beside the horse, Silver heard the voice of Murcio, of Santos, and of Christian.

The outlaw was saying: "Go straight on down the shoulder of the mountain. You'll find a pretty steep drop toward the river below. A steep drop, but they say that one wild devil of an Indian actually rode it with a horse, one day. Go down there and hunt for a boat. Look carefully. Somewhere under brush by the bank of the stream you can usually find an old rowboat or a canoe laid up. The rustlers and the smugglers leave them.

"If you find a boat, light two fires in the hollow. Small ones. They'll be enough for me to see. In half an hour I'll come out and look, and if I see the lights, I'll know that you have the boat. And I'll get the girl tied onto one of the horses. She's a lot better now. I'll take her down, and in an hour we'll be on safe soil."

"He has the moon now, Señor Christian," said the voice

of Murcio, "and with that light he will find anything that can be found."

"Unless the sight is frozen out of his head," answered Christian. "Forget about him. There is not one chance in a thousand that he is still on the trail, and a thousand-to-one trail is a long-enough shot to be worth our money, amigos."

Santos said calmly: "Now that we are in sight of the Mexico we love, I feel a calmness and a surety, Señor Christian. And if we win through, Murcio and I shall never forget what you have done. We shall never forget, Christian, that you have managed to draw us through the pinch. My own heart was water, I know! Adios for a few moments. Come, Murcio. This will be a night to talk of hereafter. The cursed wind, the cold. And most of all, how the poor Blondy lay dead on the rock! Ah! It puts more cold in me to think of that!"

Murcio and big Santos strode off.

"And all the horses?" called Santos from a little distance.

"I'll bring them all," said Christian. "Don't worry about them. I'll bring them all. The boat's the thing that we want now!"

Santos and Murcio disappeared. Their footfalls passed beyond hearing, and even the noise of their voices went out.

Then Silver came out of his hiding and entered the cave.

Those few moments of standing idle had completed the work of the cold on his body. His very knees seemed frozen stiff.

Slowly he went on, until a turn of a corner brought him blinking into view of the fire. He shrank back against the wall and stared.

He saw the girl lying on a bed of brush near the heat of the fire, wrapped in blankets, her head turning restlessly back and forth, a vague murmur coming from her lips now and then. Her face was foreshortened. It seemed to Silver like the face of a child.

Other beds of brush had been made, but that was no doubt because they had intended to spend the entire night in the cave. The falling of the wind and the clearing of the sky had been enough to bring them out for action, however.

Now that Silver was present, what could he do?

If he ventured to draw a gun, his numb fingers would make action almost impossible for him, and he could not be sure of an accurate shot unless he steadied the gun on the big boulder which lay next to the wall, and shot his man unawares.

And why not shoot him in that fashion? He dropped to his knees, laid the revolver over the edge of the boulder, and drew a careful bead.

He aimed for the heart. It was the bigger and the safer target. And centering on that goal, Silver found that there was not a tremor in his arms. He had merely to release the hammer that had been drawn back by his thumb and that famous man of crime, Barry Christian, would be no more.

Yet he could not let the hammer flick out from under the ball of his thumb. He had killed men before, but never helpless men. And now Barry Christian was on one knee beside the stretched-out body of the girl, with his slender hand laid on her forehead. There was something paternal in the position and the gesture, and the heart of Silver failed him.

He shifted his aim to the head. That pale face looked incapable of any warm human emotion. Staring at it, Silver could well imagine that the man had been guilty of all the crimes that were attributed to him. But still it was hard to fire. He shifted the aim yet higher, to the forehead.

It was a narrow brow, but it was marked and modeled by thought, as it seemed to Silver, and he dwelt on it with wonder and with respect. To shoot the man through the body—that would be a comparatively simple matter. But to send a bullet crashing through the delicate mechanism of the brain—that was far different. With a convulsive shudder Silver realized that he could not fire.

If he killed Barry Christian, it would have to be as they stood face to face!

The very thought took his breath. He tried, in desperate silence, to conquer the impulse which was controlling him, but in another moment he knew that he was enslaved by it. He would have to stand before Barry Christian and endure that unendurable eye, and stare into that pale face, and wait for the action of that slender hand.

Silver, slipping the revolver back into its spring holster under his arm, began with powerful fingers to knead the muscles of his right forearm and his wrist. He passed his hand up to the shoulder, still working at the flesh. It did not matter what the condition of the rest of his body might be. What counted was no more than the freedom and the strength of his right arm, for the ordeal that must come.

A shadow swept down the cavern. It was Barry Christian who had risen and was walking down the length of the cave. Silver, rising, covered him with the Colt.

He had dreamed that Christian would make a flashing movement to get at a gun, and that movement would be Christian's passport to another world. But he was wrong. For an instant, halted in mid-stride, Christian balanced on his toes, as though he were contemplating hurling himself straight at the enemy. Then he settled back on his heels and nodded.

"It's Silver, I suppose?" said he.

"It is," said Silver.

"Before you put the bullet through me, Silver, let me have a look again at the face of the man who's to kill me, will you?"

He moved back, as he spoke, putting his hands on his hips as though to give mute assurance that he would attempt no sudden effort to get at a weapon.

Silver followed.

They stood on opposite sides of the fire, considering one another as two men in this world have rarely surveyed enemies.

Silver said: "I might as well make you easy, Christian. I'm not going to murder you."

"Ah, and certainly not," said the soft voice of Christian. "It isn't murder but the act of justice, long delayed."

"No," said Silver. "It may be justice, but I'm not the fellow who can be judge and jury and hangman, all at once. We'll fight this out, Christian, with a fair break for both of us."

"A fair break? Your gun in your hand and an invitation for me to go for mine—to fill my hand before I die. Well, that's the ripe old Western custom, at that."

Slowly Silver shook his head.

"I don't mean that," he said. "I've got to keep you covered until my right arm thaws out. I'm a little chilled Christian. But when the life is back in my right hand, I'll put up this gun, and we'll start from an even break."

"Ah, Silver," said Christian, "you're an honest man! You're so honest that I could almost trust you to mean everything that you say."

He flung out one of his hands to the side as he said this. And the horses which stood along the side of the cave tossed up their heads. They made Silver think of the great stallion which stood outside in the snow.

Then the voice of the girl broke in rapidly: "Keep climbing till you get to the heart of the whirlwind, where the ice is. Keep climbing. The cold takes you by the throat. Keep climbing. Then you come to a turn. I don't know whether it's right or left. You come to a turn. After that there is fire and rest. You have to climb up. You have to keep on climbing—"

Silver indicated her with a pointing finger. And the great Barry Christian nodded.

"I know," he said. "That's the reason why I have to die."

"Are you ready?" said Silver.

"Yes," said Christian.

He began to smile in a singular small way, while his eyes ran eagerly over and over the face of Silver, as though he had to read it thoroughly and learn it by heart, because it was a thing that soon would be seen no more.

An active chill of dread worked like worms of ice through the spinal marrow of Silver, for he knew that to Christian the battle was already as good as ended. The sublime self-confidence of this man was like a tower of brass that no force in the world could budge.

"Very well," said Silver. He slid the gun he held into the spring holster that was under his left armpit.

"That's the way," said Christian. "Much better than a hip holster, eh?"

"Much better." agreed Silver, steadily looking into the strange eyes of Christian.

Christian threw back his head, and the long hair lifted a little over his shoulders.

"And when they ask for 'Hands up,' if they see your hands go up past the hip holsters, they're not expecting a draw from under the coat, eh?"

Silver said nothing.

"I'll look at the girl first," said Christian. "Perhaps I can do something for her comfort before we have the little fight over."

It was a lie, and Silver suddenly recognized the lie. It was not about the girl that Christian was thinking, but of some device by which he could gain an advantage. And that was why Silver watched and waited, and strung his nerves on a hair trigger. That was why he noted, as Christian turned, leaning a little over the girl in the bed, that the hand of the outlaw was moving, his right shoulder hunching up a trifle. At that very moment, as he turned his back, Christian was drawing his gun, and then he would spin swiftly to—

It was exactly so. As a frightened cat turns, so did Christian. His hand was a flash of white. His revolver was a flash of steel-blue light. But Silver had moved, also. And his gesture was like the snapping end of a whiplash. On the tips of his flying fingers the heavy Colt seemed to come forth, with the thumb jerking across the hammer.

The guns exploded, but Silver's a fraction of a second first. He knew he had won. He knew it by the fact that the weapon in Christian's hand was a trifle out of line. Therefore the spurt of fire was not a finger aimed at the heart of Silver. Instead, the bullet struck one of the line of mustangs and ripped through the haunch of the poor beast. And Silver's bullet, striking the gun from Christian's hand, flung it back against his breast, unbalanced him, and sent him sprawling backward.

That fall was why the second shot from Silver's gun missed the forehead of his enemy.

He heard the cry; he saw the astonished face of Christian, staring as though at a ghost. And as the man fell, the wounded mustang leaped straight across the fire, stumbled, kicked a shower of flaming brands in all directions, and drew with it the rest of the horses in a whirling mill.

What happened to Christian became of no moment for the instant. Silver sprang for the girl and caught her up out of harm's way as the mill of wheeling horses straightened out and bolted for the mouth of the cave.

Over that thunder of snorting, of stamping, of pounding hoofs, he heard the quiet voice of the girl saying:

"To keep on climbing—you get to the heart of the whirlwind, where the ice is. Keep on climbing—"

She spoke calmly, and her glance rested on his face with a grave abstraction. Silver put her back on one of the heaps of brush that had been laid down for a bed. Christian was not there in the cave. Christian was gone!

XIX

The Avalanche

He had thought that the great outlaw must surely have been trampled into the ground by the hammering hoofs of the fear-maddened mustangs, but Christian was gone—crouching, perhaps, just outside the cave mouth, or around the curve of the wall.

There was no time to feel fear or to hold back. Silver ran like a madman out of the cave into the icy breath of the outer night—right out across the shoulder of the mountain, where the stars seemed to be sweeping in toward his face. The horses were in full flight still, crashing around the side of the mountain to the right. But off to the left he thought he saw a smaller shadow, and heard a smaller sound.

From the edge of the shoulder of the mountain he looked down and saw the figure descending, a shadow picked out by starlight against the white sheen of the snow. He fired. The form disappeared.

Silver craned his neck and tilted his head to listen to the fall of the body, and waited to see it appear again, caroming down the slope like a loosened stone, for the angle of the descent was extremely sharp.

But he heard no fall; he saw no loose, bouncing body. Only, in the valley beneath him, he marked two small red eyes, where fires had been lighted, side by side.

Murcio and Santos were down there, then, beside a boat that was ready to cross the stream. And now, far, far down the slope, he saw a flying shadow—a man running, sliding—Christian, hastening on his way to freedom.

And no human being could on foot make up the ground that the man had gained!

But Christian had said that a wild Indian once rode his mustang down that slope!

135

Where a mustang could go by sunlight, Parade could follow by the moon. Where a mustang could go in full summer, Parade could follow over the winter snows. Cat-footed, eagle-eyed, it was not for nothing that he had run wild in his youth over the Sierra Blanca, and for Silver he would give the heart out of his body unhesitatingly.

If only he were now fit and well and strong!

But as he stood, he was the one engine that could carry Silver onto his quarry. And remembering that pale face of Christian, that strange eye, it seemed to Silver that half the evil in the world was concentrated in the monster.

He ran like mad to the stallion. Before he was in the saddle, Parade was crouching, trembling for the start. One electric flash of sympathy leaped between them and made them a unit as Silver headed him across the shoulder and to the head of the long devil's slide that descended with few breaks toward the river far beneath them.

If the snow were firmly crusted—if it did not start into an avalanche!

He put the big horse at the brink of the slope. Parade thrust his head out and down, read his task like a mountain goat, and then tipped over the edge.

Nothing could stop him after that. Irresistible force of gravity dragged him down with increasing speed. He threw up his forehoofs again and again, and stamped them down into the snow. It loosened, skidded. They began to swerve to the side—once fully sidewise, they would topple over and over, and come in a red mass of ruin to the bottom of the pitch.

Silver threw his weight far to the other side. As though he were bearing on a rudder when a boat is in a strong current, he felt the chestnut right himself. Behind them there was a roar like a rising wind, though the only breath of wind was the sweeping current of the gale that the speed of the horse raised, the storm that seemed to be blowing the stars straight up into the sky faster and faster.

Silver looked back. What he saw looked like a dozen white horses galloping close together, with manes flying high. It was the forefront of an avalanche that he had started in his own descent with Parade, and now it came after him springing, vaulting, gathering headway and width of front. He veered Parade to the side, swaying his own body. He looked back again, and twenty more white horses were plunging downward on an ever-broadening front.

Well to the side he drew. There was a rushing that seemed to fill all the air about him. A spray of powdered snow struck him like the wings of gigantic moths beating impalpably, but with weight. He was covered by a swirl of ruin. Then the thing cleared, and to his right lay the dark path of the snow slide, and in front of him it roared on its way, leaving the ground swept and dug clean behind.

In the scar that it had left, Parade went nimbly, securely down the step as the avalanche reached the river and rushed far out into it.

The waters dashed up in a mad white tumult. Then the sound smote the ears of Silver like the booming of a volley of great guns, and afterward there were the roaring echoes that thundered up and down the ravine.

He could look at something except his own progress down the hillside now. He could see the boat put out from the shore with three men in it. He could see the swirl which the avalanche had started in the river catch hold of the skiff and start it spinning helplessly, borne rapidly down the stream.

Another sound reached him, thin and small as the crying of sea birds on a wind, and he knew that it was the screaming of the frightened Mexicans in the boat as they were carried down toward the cataract.

Silver himself braced out along the shore of the stream on the back of Parade.

All was confusion in the little boat.

He saw two men rise in it. One was Santos; the slender form was Christian. And then Alonso Santos dropped.

He fell over the gunwale. Christian took his legs and upended them. That was the end of Alonso Santos, gentleman, borne like a log down toward the white thrashing of the cataract.

Now Christian was himself at the oars, bending his back almost double with effort. Murcio, also, in the bow of the boat, was laboring, his head blindly down as he strained.

Either it was the brain or the hand of Christian that aided, or else the great swirl that had caught them had now diminished in strength, for the boat no longer spun about. It straightened. It pointed its prow for the farther shore.

Murcio stopped rowing for an instant and pointed

toward the nearest bank. Silver knew what his plea was—
to turn back to the nearer bank and gain it before the
sweep of the river had them among the rocks. And Silver
knew why Christian would not turn back—for when he
landed it would be under the guns of his enemy. Death or
freedom for Christian now, it seemed!

They went on rapidly across the stream, the oars striking in steady time. But they gained less and less steadily,
and the roar of the cataract, as Silver followed down the
stream, deafened him. The cliffs above took up the sound
and hurled it back and down. Exactly like a deluge of
thunder it fell from the sky.

They had ceased gaining. They were pointing the nose
of the boat up the stream, and even so the draw of the
shooting current pulled them slowly down!

They began to go with redoubled speed. Silver saw the
head of Murcio tip back. He could guess the agony on
that fat, evil face as the man fought against sure death.
And there was the great Christian throwing the oars from
him, rising in the stern of the boat, his arms folded, his
long hair blown back from his head, meeting the last moment like a man.

Another thought seemed to strike the outlaw. He turned
and waved his hand in farewell to the enemy who had
driven him to the last disaster.

Silver, by that time, had ridden into the stream so far
that the swift water was boiling above the stirrups. Now
he whirled the heavy rawhide lariat around his head as he
plucked it off the saddlebows. With all his might he flung
it. Like liquid lead the weighty coils shot out. The small
noose darted like the head of a snake and struck the
moon-silvered water—feet short of the mark!

But not too short for Christian to make one final effort.
From the gunwale of the boat he leaped with all his might
and struck the face of the river on the very brink of the
place where the cataract kept flinging up its insane, white
arms.

Had he reached the end of the lariat?

Murcio shot into the white mist. The last Silver saw of
him, the Mexican had dropped his oars and thrown both
arms up above his head. It was a gesture of utter terror
and despair, as though on the brink of death he saw all
hell opening before him.

Then, on Silver's rope, came a heavy tug that staggered

Parade. He turned the horse and rode the stallion up the bank of the stream. He looked back, and there saw something like a long, dark fish being drawn into the shallows.

It was a limp, half-lifeless body that Silver drew out of the river. There was no strength left except in the hands of Christian, which had frozen a mighty grip on that meager little loop of salvation.

Afterward he sat up with a sudden sigh and looked up into the face of Silver with strange, unfathomable eyes.

His voice was as soft and calm as though he had been sitting all his while at a dinner table.

"It was the silly little trick, Silver," he said. "I should not have pretended about the girl. It gave you a tenth part of a second to read my mind, and a tenth part of a second is a long, long time for such a man as you. Long enough, Silver, to take a soul to heaven—or to hell with poor Murcio, and that Santos!"

They spent three days up in the cave nursing the girl. During that time Christian seemed to identify himself perfectly with the interests of his captors. In fact, from the moment when he was taken out of the water, he spoke a bitter word only once. That was right at the end.

When the three days were up, the fever left the girl as quickly as it had taken her, and they started back by slow marches. Time was of no importance, so they went edging along the river in easy stages until they reached the town of Medinos. That was where the law gathered them in.

It wanted the girl and Jim Silver as witnesses. It wanted Rap Brender to lodge behind the bars on several counts. But, above all, it wanted Barry Christian.

To a great many people the excitement began only then, in the time when two strong posses entered the region over which Barry Christian had been as a king and overthrew his reign. They hauled in plenty of crooks who were wanted in all parts of the country, but for every one captured, ten dispersed. Not without fighting. There were two or three pitched battles, but without a leader, the outlaws could not trust one another. The whole range was cleaned out in surprisingly short order.

But when the first outfit of hard riders reached the oasis of Tom Higgins, they found on it nothing but the Mexicans—who knew nothing! Higgins was gone. Stew and his fellow gunman had disappeared, transported, in spite of their wounds, no one could say where. The clever old brain of Doc Shore had attended to those details. And Doc Shore himself had dissolved just like morning mist.

Copper Creek needed the ·burning of some gunpowder before it was cleaned out. There was one item that Jim Silver had asked for and which was brought back to him, and that was a gold watch out of the stock of Shore's shop. It was the gold watch on the back of which Butch Lawson had carved the scroll with the point of his knife, that scroll which was to Shore as a message that said "Kill the bearer!" Silver looked for a long time on that scroll when he received the watch.

· Judge Brender had come down for the trials of Rap and Christian. He said to Jim Silver:

"What did you think when Lawson did that to the watch and gave it to you?"

"I thought there was one chance in two that it had nothing to do with me," said Silver.

"Why take an even chance for the sake of a dirty crook?" asked Brender.

The reply of Silver was a memorable one that was widely repeated at the time. He said:

"You see, Lawson was not a crook just then; he was only a dying man."

By the time the trial of Rap Brender came on, public opinion had been pretty well informed as to what had happened, and public opinion demanded an acquittal. If the law had an honest hold on the life and the fortunes of Rap, it had not the slightest chance to exert an influence for the good reason that in the courtroom sat Rap's father, his mother, the girl, and, above all, Jim Silver. There is one thing they understand in the West, and that is friendship. Every man and woman in that courtroom knew what Silver and Brender had done for one another.

The judge, though he kept his face like iron all during the trial, at the end of it delivered to the jury a charge that was really shameful, for he said that such a true narrative as that of the heroism and self-sacrifice of Brender and Jim Silver was better for the youth of the nation than all the moralizing in books, and that every man in the West would stand inches straighter because he knew what a friend could and ought to be.

Then the jury walked out of the box, walked back again, and by its smiling its verdict was known. The judge smiled, also.

Then came two events in rapid succession—the disappearance of Jim Silver and the marriage of the girl with Rap Brender. Of course, Silver was to stand as best man, but as the wedding couple waited in the hotel to start for the little church through streets lined with a thousand excited cow-punchers drawn from distances of a hundred miles, a note was brought to Rap, and when he opened it he read aloud:

"Saying good-by needs a special talent that I lack. God bless you both. I'm called north on a long errand, but one day I'll see you again—in Texas, San Nicador, or somewhere.

"JIM SILVER."

"But why?" cried the girl. "What could it be that takes him away?"

Rap Brender, considering that question with a sad face, said: "It's something in his blood. And no doctor will ever discover what. But the main reason he's gone is that we don't need him any more."

"Need him?" said the girl. "We'll always need him. We'll never be so happy that having Jim near wouldn't make us happier."

But Brender shook his head, looking old and grave.

"You don't understand," he said, and she saw that she would have to leave it at that.

Of course, the law wanted Silver's testimony against Barry Christian, but the district attorney was not foolish enough to try to pursue the rider of the chestnut stallion. And there was plenty of other testimony to offer. Witnesses flooded in from ten directions. One man had traveled five thousand miles so that he could stand up in the courtroom and say what he knew.

Barry Christian, his pale, sensitive face always in repose, listened calmly to the testimony. His lawyer offered a vague defense. There was really nothing to be said, and Barry Christian knew it. He was as calm as ever when he heard the jury's verdict, and also later, when he was sentenced to be hanged.

Afterward a curious reporter said to Christian: "What did Jim Silver get out of all this riding and fighting, and taking his life in his own hands?"

Christian answered: "He got the knowledge that he'd gained a friend, and that I would have a chance to think things over. No one minds dying. It's the death house that counts."

That was characteristic of Christian. He was big enough and calm enough even to confess his own fears!

And Jim Silver?

On the day when the judge sentenced Barry Christian, Silver was far, far to the north, halting Parade at the mouth of a pass that overpeered a sweep of desolate mountains, far above the timber line. But there was a smile on the lips of Silver. The thrilling cold of the wind washed the soul of the man clean. It made him as free as the wild ducks which, in a dim, gray wedge, were hurling north above him, with the song of their freedom reaching the earth as a melancholy music.

Max Brand® is the best known pen name of Frederick Faust, creator of Dr Kildare™, Destry, and many other fictional characters popular with readers and viewers worldwide. Faust wrote for a variety of audiences in many genres. His enormous output totalling approximately thirty million words or the equivalent of 530 ordinary books, covered nearly every field: crime, fantasy, historical romance, espionage, Westerns, science fiction, adventure, animal stories, love, war, and fashionable society, big business and big medicine. Eighty motion pictures have been based on his work along with many radio and television programs. For good measure he also published four volumes of poetry. Perhaps no other author has reached more people in more different ways.

Born in Seattle in 1892, orphaned early, Faust grew up in the rural San Joaquin Valley of California. At Berkeley he became a student rebel and one-man literary movement, contributing prodigiously to all campus publications. Denied a degree because of unconventional conduct, he embarked on a series of adventures culminating in New York City where, after a period of near starvation, he received simultaneous recognition as a serious poet and successful popular-prose writer. Later, he traveled widely, making his home in New York, then in Florence, and finally in Los Angeles.

Once the United States entered the Second World War, Faust abandoned his lucrative writing career and his work as a screenwriter to serve as a war correspondent with the infantry in Italy, despite his fifty-one years and a bad heart. He was killed during a night attack on a hilltop village held by the German army. New books based on magazine serials or unpublished manuscripts continue to appear. Alive and dead he has averaged a new one every four months for seventy-five years. In the U.S. alone nine publishers issue his work, plus many more in foreign countries. Yet, only recently have the full dimensions of this extraordinarily versatile and prolific writer come to be recognized and his stature as a protean literary figure in the 20th Century acknowledged. His popularity continues to grow throughout the world.